Mommies

By

Graysen Morgen

2015

Mommies © 2015 Graysen Morgen
Triplicity Publishing, LLC

ISBN-13: 978-0996899444
ISBN-10: 0996899448

Printed in the United States of America

First Edition – 2015
Cover Design: Triplicity Publishing, LLC
Interior Design: Triplicity Publishing, LLC
Editor: Jessica Roth - Triplicity Publishing, LLC

Also by Graysen Morgen

Meant to Be

Coming Home

Brides (Bridal Series book 2)

Bridesmaid of Honor (Bridal Series book 1)

Crashing Waves

Cypress Lake

Falling Snow

Fast Pitch

Fate vs. Destiny

In Love, at War

Just Me

Love, Loss, Revenge

Natural Instinct

Secluded Heart

Submerged

Acknowledgements

Special thanks to my editor, Jessica Roth for weeding through my chaos. I know it wasn't easy! *Multas gratias!*

Dedication

This book is dedicated to my wife, the person who is my everything. Thank you for making me a mommy. *Te amo semper.*

Chapter 1

The dark gray Porsche sports car whipped into the parking lot, screeching to a halt in one of the spaces on the side of the small building. The driver swung the door open. White and blue diamonds in the platinum band on her left hand glistened in the bright afternoon sun. She slid on her sunglasses as she stepped out into the scorching heat, her chestnut hair hanging in loose waves around her shoulders. Her black pantsuit and low-cut, light pink blouse accentuated the subtle curves of her athletic frame and perky breasts as she walked across the parking lot.

"How did I get so lucky?" Daphne said with a smile. The blue and white diamonds of her vintage ring glimmered as she tucked a loose strand of chin-length blond hair behind her ear. Simply looking at her beautiful wife had made her weak in the knees since she was fifteen years old.

"I have no idea," Britton replied with a grin, kissing her softly before sliding into the seat across from her.

They'd been married nearly a year and a half, after a few crazy months of dating and a spontaneous wedding, and so far it had been nothing but wedded bliss. Britton's architectural design company was thriving and Daphne was enjoying her promotion at the new

Kingstown Distribution Center for Prescott Grocery, the company Britton's family had founded over a hundred years ago.

"I like that I get to have lunch with you whenever I want." Daphne beamed.

"Does that include afternoon delight?" Britton teased.

Daphne shook her head and laughed. "I'd never make it back to the office and your dad is coming in for a meeting later."

Britton shrugged. "He's your father-in-law. I'm sure he'll understand if you're a little late."

"You're trouble."

"So you keep telling me."

Britton picked up the menu and perused the lunch section. It didn't matter where she was or what she was doing, as long as she got to spend time with her wife. She never thought she was capable of loving anyone as much as she loved the woman sitting across from her.

"I talked to Bridget this morning. She didn't sound too happy with you."

"My sister always has a thorn in her side where I'm concerned because I don't conform to the lifestyle of the rich and famous like she and my mother do. What's up her ass this time?" Britton asked, flipping the menu over.

Daphne shrugged. "She mentioned something about your mom, but I had another call coming in, so I had to let her go."

Britton pursed her lips. "She and Wade have been married over two years. Mom's been hounding her about having kids and she thinks that's my fault."

2

"Well, you did make your mom think she was pregnant, which got a rise out of your mom at your sister's expense."

Britton laughed. "Yeah, that was fun while it lasted."

"I'm not getting between the two of you. She's my best friend and you're my wife, so you're on your own with this one. Cut her some slack, though. I know what it's like to have your mother constantly asking questions."

Britton set her menu aside. "What kind of questions?"

"I'm an only child, Britton. My mother wants grandkids as bad as yours does."

"Wonderful," Britton muttered, waving the waiter over to order a salad. She was about to say something else when her cell phone rang. She pulled it from her jacket pocket and showed Daphne the picture of her mother on the caller ID.

"Are you going to answer it?" Daphne asked, before ordering a wrap.

"No. She can leave a voicemail. I'm sure it's something stupid anyway. She called me a few days ago to ask me if I wanted her china set. She's either going through a late midlife crisis or updating her will, neither of which I care to discuss with her right now."

"I don't blame you," Daphne replied with a soft smile, allowing her eyes to linger.

"Did you invite me or my breasts to lunch?" Britton teased.

"What?" Daphne fumbled.

"Don't say I didn't offer—"

3

"I heard you the first time," Daphne interjected, shaking her head to hide her grin.

Their lunch appeared and the playful conversation ended as they quickly ate.

~

Sitting in the downtown traffic, Britton remembered her mother's call. She quickly pressed the Bluetooth button on the steering wheel, listening to the voicemail.

Darling, I'm calling to invite you and Daphne to Sunday brunch. Please let me know as soon as you can, so I can plan accordingly. Love you.

"Great," Britton sighed. She'd thought when she finally got married, her parents would butt out of her life, but they seemed to be more involved than ever.

She pulled her sports car into the parking lot and walked into the office building that housed her design company.

"Mr. Mayor?" she said, holding a hand out to the man sitting in a chair near the receptionist's desk. "I wasn't expecting you," she added. "Come into my office." In truth, she never thought she'd see him again after turning down his advances and revealing she was a lesbian. That was before he left Cranston to become the Mayor of Providence.

"I know you weren't, but I was in the area and wanted to talk to you in person," he replied, following her into the large room to the right. "Governor Mitchum is looking to add a new modern art museum to the state. I'm pushing to get it here in Providence."

"That's great," she exclaimed, sitting behind her metal-framed desk with a glass top as he sat across from her.

"I'm also going to recommend that you design it."

"Wow. Even better." She smiled.

"I'm giving you a heads up because we're meeting next week and he could have a decision by then on the city, so I need to be ready to run with the project. I'll go over the budget and have my assistant send you the figures."

"That doesn't give me much time, but I'm sure I can throw some rough sketches together." Britton pulled a notepad from one of her side drawers. "What square footage are we looking at and how many floors?"

The Mayor shrugged. "It's probably going to be two floors and maybe 6,000 square feet, nothing huge, but big enough for modern art displays and a traveling exhibit or two."

"I'll get on it today," Britton replied, taking notes. "I should have the preliminary design ready for your meeting with him. Keep in mind it'll be rough sketches, so there will be a lot of wiggle room."

"Sounds great. I'll have the details to you by Monday."

Britton shook his hand and walked him out.

"What was that about?" Kathleen, her assistant, said as she stepped up next to her.

"I have no idea. I thought that pencil dick hated me." Britton shook her head. "Have you heard anything about a new modern art museum?"

"Nope. Does he want you to design it?"

"Either that or he's going to be a huge waste of my time," she sighed. "I guess we'll see."

"On another note, the contractor for the Hardy Sporting Goods building called this morning. He's estimating that they're a week to ten days ahead of schedule."

"Really?"

"Yes. I was surprised, too."

"All right. Don't call Thomas Hardy until the inspection is scheduled. We don't want to get burned if that backfires on us. The grand opening is planned for four weeks from now. If it gets done early, that's great. It'll give them more time to put the up the shelving and get it ready for inventory."

"Sounds good. How was lunch?"

Britton grinned, thinking about Daphne. "Wish I didn't have to go back to work," she called over her shoulder as she walked away.

Chapter 2

Later that evening, Britton pulled through the wrought iron gate in front of her large, two-story, European-style home. She parked her car in the garage next to Daphne's black Mercedes, and walked inside the place they called home.

The aroma of dinner wafted through the air as Britton walked through the laundry room and down the hallway.

"Something smells divine," she called out, shedding her jacket as she stepped into the open kitchen and pulled her blouse free of her waistband.

"Takeout. I didn't feel like cooking," Daphne replied with her head in the refrigerator. She turned around, nearly dropping the chilled bottle of wine she was holding as her eyes landed on Britton, leaning against the counter on the opposite side of the island, undoing the last of the buttons on her blouse. She tugged it open, revealing her nude-colored, satin bra and naturally tanned skin. "Must you get undressed in the kitchen every day?" she murmured, shaking her head.

The food on the dining table was forgotten as Britton wiggled out of her shirt and placed it on the island next to her jacket. Daphne was in her arms with their lips pressed together in a heated kiss before she could take another step. Britton broke the kiss long enough to pull Daphne's shirt over her head.

Both women worked simultaneously, releasing the buttons, zippers, and clasps between them, until they were naked. Their bodies melded together, feeling the warm sensation of soft skin on skin. They rocked gently against the counter as their hands dipped lower, finding the sweet spot each had been languidly searching for. Trading sultry kisses, they slowly touched each other, neither in a hurry to bring the euphoric sensation to an end.

There was nothing Britton desired more than being in this moment, feeling Daphne inside and out as she made love to her. It was the highest of highs, a place she never wanted to come down from.

Daphne finally pulled her mouth away from Britton's lips, gasping for air as her body began to betray her, releasing her climax all on its own. Britton grinned and held her close as Daphne's body trembled against her. It only took one extra stroke for her to let go as well. They leaned against the counter on wobbly legs, smiling as their bodies slowly returned to normal.

"I thought this would stop once we moved in together," Daphne murmured, nuzzling her head on the crook of Britton's neck.

"You started it," Britton laughed.

Daphne smiled and shook her head as she pushed away from her. "Stop stripping in the kitchen and maybe one night we'll have a dinner that isn't cold or burned," she chided.

Britton shrugged sheepishly and gathered her clothes. Her stomach growled as the scent of Chinese takeout filled her nostrils when she passed by the dining room.

~

The dining table was cleared of the empty containers as Britton and Daphne curled up on the couch in the den, both sexually satisfied, with sated stomachs. Britton clicked on the TV and Daphne reached for the remote in her hand.

Britton growled like a small dog and held the controller out of her reach.

"I love you with everything that I am, and your nerdy side is sexy as hell, but if you make me watch one more historic documentary, I'm going to shave my head!" Daphne exclaimed, climbing on top of her to grab the remote.

"Why is your hair involved in this?" Britton laughed, still trying to hold it out of her reach.

"Because, that's the one thing you limit," Daphne replied.

"Fine, shave it. It'll grow back," Britton teased.

Refusing to give up, Daphne began tickling Britton's sensitive sides until she could no longer hold her arm up, giving up the controller and retreating to the other end of the couch like a sad puppy as Daphne moved off her lap.

"We've been summoned to Sunday brunch," Britton muttered as she watched the channels scroll on the TV.

"I promised my mom I'd go to that home and garden thing downtown."

"Guess I'm going alone," Britton yawned.

"What's she got up her sleeve this time?" Daphne asked, finally landing on a movie they both liked.

"Who knows? Oh, I almost forgot, the mayor stopped by the office today."

"Really? That's a shock considering how homophobic he is."

"I know," Britton agreed. "Anyway, the governor wants to build a new modern art museum and he's trying to get it here. He wants me to put something together for their meeting next week."

"Don't you need more time than that?"

"Yes, but I told him I'd get some rough sketches done." She kicked her feet up onto the coffee table. "I'm not putting a lot of time into it until I know it's open for bidding. Dealing with municipalities is a pain in the ass. They want it done as quickly and cheaply as possible, yet they take forever to approve anything."

"Are you going to try to get the job?"

"Sure. It doesn't hurt to throw some sketches together and put a bid in, but I'm not going to break my back for something that may never happen. Besides, Senator Ferguson should be approving the model of his summer home soon."

"Do you think you'll do more residential contracts, or stay mostly with commercial?" Daphne questioned, turning to put her feet up between them with her elbow on the back of the cushions. She leaned over, placing her chin in her hand.

"I honestly don't know. This house was the only residential drawing I'd ever done, until he asked me to design that English cottage for his family. I guess we'll see where it goes. The company is doing well, growing by leaps and bounds, but I'm not really at the point where

I can turn down a job or simply not put a bid in on something. I love my dad and I'm thankful for everything he's done for me, but the sooner I sever this agreement, the better."

"I've never heard him say anything about the silent partnership."

"He hasn't, well not in front of you, anyway. We had a discussion during tax season, haven't spoken about it since. He knows I'm paying back his personal investment before the loan from my trust fund. I probably have another year and a half, maybe two, before I'm free and clear of everything. The more business I bring in, the sooner I get to that point," Britton said, pulling Daphne's feet into her lap as she began to massage them.

"That feels good," Daphne murmured.

Britton looked longingly at her. They'd fallen so easily into domestic life. She often had a difficult time conjuring up what her life was like before Daphne had appeared, ready to scratch her eyes out. She remembered how they used to despise one another and smiled, thinking it was comical, especially knowing how much they loved each other.

"What?" Daphne asked, watching the emotions roll across her wife's face as her expression changed. "Do you need me to cancel with my mom?"

"Huh? No." Britton shook her head. "I was just thinking back to when you used to hate me."

Daphne rolled her eyes. "I never hated you. I hated the fact that I wanted you more than a dehydrated animal wants water."

Britton pushed Daphne's feet aside and crawled over to her, squeezing herself between Daphne and the couch cushions. "I love you," she whispered, kissing her softly.

"I love you too," Daphne replied, running her hand through the long, chestnut waves that cascaded over Britton's shoulders.

"I wouldn't change the last year." Britton put her head on Daphne's chest, listening to her heartbeat.

"Really? Not even the time we got food poisoning from that new place you said we had to go to?"

Britton laughed. "No. There's nothing like bonding as a newly married couple while puking next to each other.

"Or worse," Daphne chuckled, wrapping her arms around Britton.

Chapter 3

Sharon Prescott was sitting in the solarium, sipping a peach and cranberry Bellini when her daughter walked in, alone. "Where's Daphne?" she asked, looking around.

"She already had plans with her mother. They were going to some kind of home and garden show," Britton replied, sitting down adjacent to her mother and pouring herself a drink from the iced pitcher. "Where's dad?"

"In the study as usual. I told him to join us in a little bit."

Britton nodded. A hundred scenarios were running through her head, but the light alcohol in the drink helped mellow her nerves. "What's going on, mom?"

"Can't I enjoy a nice brunch with my youngest daughter? It seems like I never see you anymore, and I rarely see Daphne. I think I actually saw you both more when you hated each other." She smiled.

Britton leaned back in her chair, folding her arms as an odd expression crossed her face.

"Have you talked to your sister lately?"

Ah ha! She thought, shaking her head. "No. Daphne talks to her a lot though."

"I'm worried about her. I think she and Wade may be having marital problems."

"What? Why would you think that?"

"She's been avoiding me and that's not like her."

"Did you piss her off?"

"Britton!" Sharon scolded.

Britton rolled her eyes. "Well?"

"No. I was questioning when she and Wade planned on settling down. She's going to be thirty soon."

"I'm assuming you're referring to kids."

"Of course. I thought for sure they had started trying right away. The fact that they didn't leads me to believe something else is going on."

"You brought me here to discuss Bridget's sex life?" Britton laughed.

"Absolutely not." Her mother shook her head. "I simply wanted to know if she'd mentioned anything to you or Daphne. Maybe you could give her a call and find out how things are going."

Britton swallowed the rest of her drink in one long sip. "She doesn't talk to me, not like that."

"Well, have Daphne do it. You'd think if she talked to anyone, it would be her best friend."

"I'll see what I can do," Britton muttered.

"Speaking of you and Daphne…"

"Our sex life is just fine. In fact—" she hedged, wiggling her eyebrows dramatically.

"Good, Lord, Britton. I don't need the details," she huffed.

Britton laughed.

"What about children? Have you at least discussed what you're going to do?"

"Has hell frozen over?" Britton muttered.

Mommies

"Hey, darling," Stephen Prescott said, kissing his daughter's cheek as he took a seat at the table. "Where's Daphne?"

"With her mother. They already had plans," Sharon answered for her. All conversation of sex lives and grandchildren was gone from the table when she completely changed the subject. "How's work going? The last time we talked, you were working on the building for that sports store, right?"

Britton chuckled inwardly, thankful to be moving onto something besides children. She didn't have anything against them, she'd just never had that itch or maternal clock ticking that most women talk about.

~

As soon as she got into her car, Britton pushed the button on the wheel for her Bluetooth and said, "Call Heather." She pulled around the circular drive of her parent's Newport Estate house as she waited for the line to pick up.

"I was just thinking about you," Heather, her longtime best friend, answered.

"Was I naked?"

"No," she laughed.

"Just checking. You never know these days. Celebrities are coming out of the closet, changing their sex, all kinds of crazy shit is going on."

"I'm not a celebrity, but if I decide to jump the fence, you'll be the first to know," Heather joked. "Where's your wife?"

"Shopping or something."

"Ah, I see. The cat's away, so the mouse wants to play."

"I just left brunch in Newport."

"Oh, what fun. What was the topic this time?"

"Bridget's sex life."

"Are you serious?" she laughed hysterically. "What the hell would you know about that?"

"Exactly. I think my mom only invited me so she could question Daphne, but to her surprise, I showed up alone."

"Are you headed home?"

"Yeah. I have some sketches to work on that are probably going to be a complete waste of my time."

"Good, swing by. We're thinking of painting the inside of the house and I need help with the colors. Greg said he liked earth tones and left me with about thirty different color combinations."

"I think he pretends to play golf," Britton replied.

"Me too, but it gets him out of my hair for a few hours every Sunday."

"I'll be there in a few minutes. What's for lunch?"

"Didn't you just eat brunch?"

"Have you ever been to brunch at my mother's? It's usually some form of light cocktail and bagels or hard toast with disgusting spreads. I drank two Bellini's, which were mostly juice, and ate nothing."

Heather giggled. "I was about to call in an order to the deli down the street."

"Sounds great. Order me a salad with grilled chicken. I'll pick the order up on my way to your house."

~

16

After inhaling her lunch, Britton began looking at the array of colors littering Heather's dining room table. "Why are you painting?" she asked.

"I'm sick of white."

Britton nodded. Every room in her and Daphne's house was a different color, but the trim was snow white. "I like these sand colors here and those light blues, or even these browns work. Oh, this blade grass green is a vibrant color. Are you looking at doing themes in different rooms, or just paining the overall color something besides white?"

"I have no idea. I didn't think it would be such a huge endeavor and Greg's been no help."

"Well, he's a man. They generally don't get involved unless it calls for money or manual labor."

Heather guffawed. "Isn't that the truth." She picked up some of the swatches and set them back down. "What would you do? I love the way your house looks. You used earth tones didn't you?"

"Yes, most of the rooms are earth tones, but we went some darker shades for accent walls. I say do what you want. If you want multiple colors with accents that give the rooms depth, then go for it. If you want an all around color that works in every room, then do that," Britton said.

"You're not much help."

"Well, I'm an architect, not an interior designer."

"Smartass," Heather laughed. "So, why is your mom interested in Bridget's sex life all of a sudden?"

Britton rolled her eyes. "You know how she is. She expects life to continue as scheduled. Bridget and Wade have been married two and a half years. She thinks they should have one and half kids by now."

"Seriously?"

"Yep, and the fact that they don't, plus Bridget has been avoiding our mother, makes her think they're having marital problems."

"Are they?"

"Who the fuck knows? I don't get involved in her marriage and she doesn't bother me with mine. Hell, I rarely talk to her."

"What about Daphne? Surely she'd know."

"That's why mom invited *us* to brunch, but she had no idea Daphne wasn't going. She wants me to either call Bridget or get Daphne to find out what's going on."

"I'm glad I'm an only child and I know my mom wants grandkids too, but she already knows we're years away from that."

"I agree."

"Has she hounded you as well?"

"Yes, but not as bad as Bridget. She knows it's a process for us. She did ask if we'd at least started the ball rolling. I'm assuming she meant have we begun looking for a sperm donor, but I doubt I'll ever hear those two words come out of my mother's mouth."

"Yeah, I doubt it too," Heather laughed. "What are you going to do?"

"I don't know. I guess I'll talk to Daphne and see what she knows before calling my sister."

Britton's cell phone was sitting on the table when Daphne's smiling face filled the screen and began playing "Addicted" by Saving Abel.

Heather snickered, shaking her head. "That must not ring much during the day."

Britton grinned and picked up the call. "Usually it's on vibrate, even better!" she teased.

"What's vibrating?" Daphne asked on the other end of the line.

"Huh? Nothing. I'm at Heather's helping her pick out paint colors."

"How was brunch?"

"My mom thinks Bridget and Wade aren't having sex, but I assured her *we* were, well into the night last night, as a matter of fact," she said, winking at Heather.

Heather rolled her eyes as she tossed a paint swatch at her and got up to clear their trash from lunch.

"Britton, I know your mother better than you do. She does not discuss sex," Daphne replied with a hint of laughter in her voice.

"It's a long story. I'll tell you about it when I get home. How was shopping?"

"We weren't shopping. It's more of a crafts exhibit to get ideas about things to do around your house. Mom's thinking of redecorating and maybe adding a flower trellis or something to her backyard," Daphne answered.

"Did you get any ideas?"

"Yes, but they had nothing to do with decorating."

"Now you're talking. I think your naked body looks better on the couch than any accent pillow or crafty wall hanging," Britton said.

"Oh, gross. Remind me not to sit on your furniture the next time I come over," Heather grimaced.

"Please. Like you and Greg don't fornicate in more places than the bedroom. I for one know you blew him in the kitchen a couple of weeks ago…and that's only because you told me and as your best friend, I listened."

Heather rolled her eyes and smiled as she walked out of the room.

"Okay, well I'm going to back myself right out of this conversation. I'm almost home anyway," Daphne muttered.

"I'll see you soon. Love you," Britton said as she hung up.

"You two are going to spontaneously combust one day, you know that right?" Heather walked her to the door and gave her a hug.

"The honeymoon phase is still going."

"Don't come crying to me when it's over. I think you're going to be heartbroken," Heather giggled.

"Nah. There is no such thing as bed death with this lesbian." Britton grinned. "Let me know when you get your colors picked out. I'll come help, but I can't paint for shit, just so you know."

"I'm going to hire painters."

"Even better," Britton yelled as she got into her car.

Chapter 4

Daphne was sitting outside, watching two skulls rowing in the bay behind their house, when Britton stepped through the French doors.

"Do you miss it?" Daphne asked as Britton wrapped her arms around her from behind.

"Yes and no," Britton answered honestly. "I used to think about it often, especially when I needed to relieve stress, but I wouldn't change the direction my life has taken. I'm happy." She kissed Daphne's neck just below her ear, inhaling the light jasmine and lavender scent of her perfume. "What about you? You were pretty skilled in a skull yourself."

"I enjoyed it, but none of us compared to the almighty Britton Prescott," she teased, placing her arms over Britton's. "What did the queen want?"

"To talk to you, actually."

"Me?" Daphne questioned, turning in her arms.

"Yeah. She really thinks Bridget and Wade are having problems and she wanted to know what you knew. Apparently, my sister is avoiding her."

"She hasn't mentioned anything to me. What makes your mom think that?"

"They haven't procreated."

Daphne shook her head and laughed.

"I'm serious. My mother wants us to talk to Bridget and see if anything is going on."

"I honestly don't think there's anything wrong with their marriage," Daphne added, pulling away to go inside.

"I don't either, but you know my mother is not going to let this go," Britton said, following her into the house.

"I know Wade has to go out of town for some kind of work training this week. Why don't we invite her to dinner one night?"

"That's fine."

~

Two days later, Britton was upstairs changing out of her pantsuit into a pair of loose cotton pants and a tank top, when she heard the doorbell. Daphne had left her office a little early in order to prepare dinner, so she was already downstairs in the kitchen.

Britton padded down the stairs and went in search of the laughter she heard wafting through the house. Bridget and Daphne were standing next to the island in the center of the kitchen, laughing about something.

"What's so funny?" she asked.

Daphne wiped tears from her eyes as she tried to explain the significance of the wine Bridget had brought. "A guy Bridget dated in college, brought this horrible bottle of wine over one night and being the polite people we were, we pretended to love it, while he drank his beer of course."

Britton raised an eyebrow, not really getting the humor of the story.

"That poor guy wanted her so bad he bought us an entire case of it! We couldn't give the stuff away, so we wound up drinking all of it over the course of our sophomore year," Daphne chuckled.

"Who was this guy? Do I know him?" Britton asked.

"God no, the relationship lasted all of two weeks, but that damn nasty wine lasted months!"

"Why didn't you throw it out?"

"Your sister was too practical back then. We were underage and it was free booze!" Daphne laughed.

"I was looking for something to bring to dinner and ran across that same wine. I don't think I've ever seen in the store," Bridget giggled. "I had to buy it."

"And you two think I'm a nerd," Britton muttered, shaking her head.

"Dinner smells delicious. I barely had time to wolf down a small salad today. I think Daddy's off his rocker lately," Bridget said.

"What's going on?" Britton asked, as Daphne went back to the stove to finish sautéing their stir-fry chicken and vegetables.

Bridget shrugged. "He's talking about expanding west. I think it's a bad idea, but—"

"Connecticut?" Daphne interjected.

"Yeah, we were so successful going into Worcester last year, and now he's looking at Hartford."

"Really?"

"Yes, he's talking about building a Distribution Center and branching out with an array of stores all over the state."

Daphne turned off the stove and plated everyone's dinner, before carrying it to the dining table. Britton was only vaguely interested in the conversation about the family business as she began eating.

"How serious is he?" Daphne questioned. "I remember when he expanded into Massachusetts. It was a nightmare for the first year," she added, shaking her head.

"I know," Bridget sighed. "He's made a few trips down, surveying land and meeting with city officials."

"Of course they're interested, it'll bring a ton of jobs to the state, but is the company financially stable enough to roll the dice on such a large project?" Daphne said.

"I was in the meeting with him and the Financial Director a couple of weeks ago. We're well into the black for the year, so it's not much of a financial gamble, but I think we're big enough as it is. We're still privately held. If we keep expanding, we're going to wind up going public because the company will be too big."

"Have you discussed this with Daddy?" Britton interrupted.

"Well, no. It's his company."

"Yeah, but it'll be yours one day, Bridge. You need to put your opinion in the hat, too."

Bridget went to rebut, but Daphne stopped her.

"She's right. You need to think long term."

Bridget nodded.

"How's Wade?" Britton asked, making a face at Daphne to get onto the real topic.

"He's good. His job sent him to Mississippi for training on the new computer system. He hates it down there. When he called me this afternoon, he said the mosquitoes are as big as my car," she laughed.

Daphne wrinkled her face. "So, married life is still good?"

"It's fine…" Bridget eyed her suspiciously.

Britton had finished her dinner, so she pushed her plate aside. "Look, mom thinks you and Wade are having marital problems."

"What?" Bridget screeched. "What the hell would give her that idea?"

Britton raised her eyebrows and threw her hands up. "You haven't had a kid yet and you've been ignoring her."

"What? No I haven't."

Britton crossed her arms.

"Okay, maybe I have a little. You know how persistent she can be."

"Is everything okay?" Daphne asked.

"Of course it is. Wade and I are happier than ever. I love him with all of my heart." She pushed her empty plate away and folded her hands in front of her on the table. "You just heard me talking about the company. I have so much going on right now, kids are the furthest thing from my mind. Mom doesn't understand. My career has always come first…mainly because I know one day I'll be the head of the company. She doesn't see the big picture.

"Wade and I want a family one day. We both agree that one kid is plenty, but we want to be more settled first. He's probably going to get promoted down the road and when that happens, he'll have a regular desk job and not travel as much. Hopefully, by then, Daddy will have slowed down enough to keep the company on an even keel where I can keep up."

"You need to put your big girl pants on and tell all of this to mom. She's not going to bite your head off if you stand up to her. I've surely done it enough to give you an idea of how it goes," Britton said.

Daphne put her hand over Bridget's. "She's right, Bridge. It's your life. When you and Wade start a family should be your decision, not anyone else's and it shouldn't be for any other reason than you both want it," Daphne added.

"She wouldn't be so adamant about me, if you hadn't told her I was trying to get pregnant, to keep her off your back," Bridget huffed at her sister. "You guys should just have a kid. That'll shut her up."

Britton spewed the sip of water she'd just drank, all over the table. Daphne laughed and handed her a clean napkin as she changes the subject.

"Just talk to her. I'll even go with you if you want. She needs to understand that you're doing what you both want right now and you're happy. I had to do the same thing with my mother. You have to remember, they come from a different generation. Women got married and had babies, they didn't run companies."

"That's true," Bridget sighed. "I should probably get going. The traffic will be a mess going back to Providence, and Wade should be calling when he gets back to the hotel." She carried her plate to the kitchen. "Dinner was fabulous as usual. Has my sister learned to cook yet?" she teased, hugging Daphne, then Britton.

"No. If dinner is left up to her, we eat out of containers," Daphne laughed.

"Hey, it's not McDonald's! I dine at some of the finest takeout places in the state, I'll have you know." Britton frowned as Bridget walked out the door.

"I'll call my mom this week. Maybe we can do Sunday brunch," Bridget called over her shoulder.

"Sounds good," Daphne replied with a fake smile. She didn't exactly want to go, knowing how unrelenting her mother-in-law could be sometimes, but Bridget was her best friend. If she needed her, she'd be there.

"Hey, you offered," Britton laughed. "I have other things to do this weekend, so good luck to you."

"Like what?" Daphne asked, closing the front door.

"Like anything other than playing twenty questions with the queen of Rhode Island!" she exclaimed, going into the kitchen to load the dishwasher.

Daphne moved behind her, pinning her against the counter. "I can think of a few things to do," she whispered.

"See, now we're on the same page." Britton spun around, pressing her lips to Daphne's as she slid her arms around her waist.

Chapter 5

A few days later, Daphne wiped the sweat from Britton's brow and cuddled her close. They were tangled in the dark gray, bed sheets, having just spent the last hour in the throes of passion like a pair of primal lovers.

"I love you," Daphne whispered.

"I love you too," Britton murmured, kissing the sensitive spot on the inside of her wife's wrist.

"What do you think about us having a baby?" Daphne asked, running her hand through Britton's hair.

"What?" Britton coughed, unsure what to say. She didn't physically want to have a child, but the idea of having one with Daphne had crossed her mind once or twice. "Where did this come from?"

"I don't know. I guess it's been on my mind with Bridget being put on the spot. I don't want that. Starting a family should be our decision, no one else's."

"I agree." Britton locked her grays eyes on her wife. "So…" Britton sat up a little straighter. "Are we having *that* conversation?" she asked, knowing the answer. They'd skirted the subject, only talking briefly about children a time or two since they'd gotten married.

Daphne's smile widened as she placed her hand on Britton's cheek. "You know I love you, and I love our life…having a family was something I had always wanted, but wasn't sure would ever happen."

"What about now?" Britton asked softly.

"I've thought about it more and more as I get closer to thirty," she said. "I actually kept that box your mother sent us with all of the information about lesbian pregnancy, while we were on our honeymoon."

"You did?" Britton chuckled.

"I thought it might come in handy one day." Daphne shrugged.

"When were you going to tell me all of this?" Britton questioned.

"Every time someone mentions babies, you leave the room or change the subject."

Britton grabbed her hand. "It's not that I don't want a child, I've just seen kids drive a wedge between some lesbian couples, and I don't want that."

"Nothing will come between us, Britton, because we won't let it. I've never loved anyone as much as I love you, whether we have kids or not, that will never change."

"I don't know how to be a mother. There is no clock ticking inside of me, and I've never had the itch that most women get. Going through the birthing process is definitely not on my to-do list."

"If it happens, I'd like to be the one to carry it for us," Daphne said. "I don't know why. I guess I knew the birthing process was something you'd definitely not be interested in." She smiled.

Britton nodded. "You're right, but I would be right beside you every step of the way." She took a deep breath. "So, what's the next step?" she asked nervously.

"Are you serious? This is a huge decision."

"Yes," Britton replied, kissing her softly. "I love you, Daphne, and I think we will make great parents."

Daphne rolled away from her and pulled the box of brochures out of her nightstand.

"You really have been thinking about this," Britton exclaimed. "I'm sorry I made you feel like you couldn't talk to me."

"It wasn't really that." Daphne moved closer, opening the box. "I guess with our rushed engagement and wedding debacle, I just wanted this to be something we decided on our own when the time was right. I think we're both in great places with our careers, so it's been on my mind more and more. This thing with Bridget really brought it to the surface. I don't want to be in her shoes, not with my family or yours."

"I agree. Now's a good time anyway. I don't want to be old and gray when he or she is graduating from high school. Those years should be some of the best time of our lives."

"I love the way you think." Daphne smiled.

"So, what's in this box?" Britton asked.

~

Daphne spent the next ten minutes explaining how artificial insemination worked, along with choosing a sperm donor.

"This entire process seems cold. It's about as far from romantic as you can get," Britton scoffed as her stomach rolled at the mental picture. "Do you really have to go to a doctor and have him insert the frozen stuff in there?"

"According to this you do. There's also In Vetro Fertilization, but that's a much more difficult medical procedure and a last resort."

"I see." Britton nodded with raised eyebrows.

"It's this or the old fashioned way."

"You men have sex with a guy?" Britton scowled.

"Yep, and if it didn't work, we'd have to keep doing it over and over." Thinking about that idea made Daphne grimace."I am not having sex with a man, so that's off the table."

"Good, because. I'd rather chew my arm off than know you had sex with a guy."

"You never did that, did you?" Daphne asked.

Britton scrunched her face. "Hell no. I knew I was a lesbian by the time I was thirteen."

"I tried experimenting once in college," Daphne muttered. "As soon as he whipped that thing out, I ran out of his dorm room and never looked back."

Britton laughed. "I can't believe you never told me that."

"It wasn't exactly my finest moment," Daphne chuckled.

"See, if you'd have just told me you were in love with me back in high school when you kissed me, you would've avoided all of that, and we wouldn't have hated each other for ten years," Britton chided with a cocky grin.

"Uh huh." Daphne smiled and shook her head. "I couldn't handle you back then. You were wild, going through life without a care in the world. Everyone wanted you, guys and girls, and it drove me nuts. Then, when I saw you again when Heather and Bridget were both getting married, you hadn't changed a bit."

"What made you think you could handle me then?" Britton teased.

Daphne pushed Britton to her back and crawled on top of her. "I grew up. I wasn't intimidated by you anymore. All of that hatred was masking the desire burning deep inside," she said, dropping her voice to a husky tone.

"Maybe we should practice that baby-making thing." Britton pulled her down for a searing kiss.

Daphne broke the kiss and pulled away. "Okay, let me go get the turkey baster and some frozen tadpoles and we'll give it a try," she laughed.

"Oh, gross!" Britton squealed, pushing her away.

"In all seriousness, I think we should talk to the doctor and get a better idea of what is involved," Daphne said, holding Britton's gaze.

Britton smiled and nodded. "I think that's a good idea."

Chapter 6

The following Monday, Britton and Daphne sat in the waiting room of the doctor's office. Britton crunched on Tic Tacs and nervously bounced her leg.

"Are you okay?" Daphne asked.

"Fine. You?" Britton answered, tossing a few more green mints into her mouth.

"You're going to choke on those damn things," Daphne murmured, shaking her head.

"Daphne Prescott?" the nurse called, opening the side door.

"Here we go," Daphne said.

"Yep." Britton jumped up, walking behind her.

They were shown to the doctor's office, where a large desk was surrounded by degrees and what looked like vacation pictures.

"Doctor Rooney will be in shortly," the nurses stated.

"Why are we in here?" Britton questioned, as the nurse left and the door shut behind them.

"We're here for a consultation, not an exam," Daphne explained.

The door opened again before Britton could say anything else, and a woman in her early forties with short, curly dark hair stepped inside. She was wearing light blue scrubs, a white lab coat, and dark sneakers.

"I'm Doctor Pauline Rooney," she said, shaking their hands. "You must be Daphne and Britton Prescott."

They watched as the doctor took her seat on the opposite side of the desk and opened the chart she was carrying.

"So, you want to make a baby, is that correct?"

Britton was about to say something smart, but Daphne kicked her ankle. "Yes," Daphne answered.

"Well, you've come to the right place." Dr. Rooney smiled. "I specialize in fertility, as well as obstetrics mostly for lesbian couples. Our office sees a number of straight patients as well, of course. My personal success rate is over seventy-five percent," she stated her normal lines as she read through their chart.

"Britton Prescott...are you the architect who designed Hardy Sporting Goods for Thomas Hardy?"

"Yes." Britton nodded.

"That's my father-in-law. He boasts about your design to everyone he meets," she laughed "You probably met my wife, Sherri. She's his right-hand man, so to speak."

Britton tried to remember the name.

"Blonde hair, big boobs, legs for days," the doctor added, causing Britton to laugh.

"I think I met her in the first meeting, but after that I only saw Mr. Hardy."

"Great people. They're over the moon with excitement for this new store." She grabbed a pen and held it over the open area at the bottom of the page for her notes. "Well, let's get down to it, shall we? Daphne, you're planning on carrying, correct?"

"Yes."

"How are your monthly cycles?"

"Normal, I guess, never heavy and only last about three or four days."

"Are they regular? Every twenty-eight days?"

Daphne nodded.

"Okay. Your medical history looks good, so there is nothing to worry about there. Are you using a known donor?"

"No," Britton squeaked.

"We're going through a sperm bank, but haven't chosen anyone yet," Daphne answered.

"We have a few that we work with often, so I'll make sure you get their contacts. It's fairly easy actually. Everything is online, so you can read profiles and even look at pictures of thousands of donors. Some of them even list how many births have occurred using particular donors. The law doesn't allow more than ten per donor, so if one has maybe seven or eight, you might want to move to someone else because when the time comes, that donor may no longer be available."

Britton looked at Daphne like a deer in the headlights. Daphne smiled softly and grabbed her hand.

"Once you chose a donor, it's really just a waiting game until your cycle comes around. Artificial Insemination is fairly easy. It can be somewhat uncomfortable, but we try to do it as quickly as possible. Based on your cycles, we'll try to pinpoint your ovulation schedule. You'll get a kit with small sticks that look like pregnancy tests. Five days before the start of the ovulation cycle, you'll begin peeing on a stick every other day. When it turns blue, you've begun the process. That's when you call the office and we get you in here for the procedure, which takes all of ten minutes. We'll order the sperm a week ahead of time, so that we have it readily available. We have a cryogenic freezer to store it in, so we're able to keep it for weeks with no issues. Do you have any questions?" Dr. Rooney asked.

Britton's mouth opened, but nothing came out.

"No. I think you've given us a lot of information. We've sort of starting researching everything, so we're getting more familiar with how it all works."

"Great." She pulled a smart chart that looked like a wheel, from her desk. "Since you're fairly regular, you can expect to ovulate sometime around 10 to 14 days after your period starts. Since it's due to start soon, we could potentially inseminate this next cycle, but you'll need to get your donor chosen, so that we can get the order placed as soon as possible. Either way, as soon you get that done, let us know what cycle you'd like to start."

"Okay," Daphne replied.

"It was nice meeting you both. I look forward to helping you make a baby." She smiled. "My assistant will give you the sperm bank information on the way out, as well as the ovulation kit. Please give our office a call if you have any questions."

As soon as they walked outside, Britton stated, "I don't want anyone to know we're doing this. At least not right away."

"I agree. This is between you and me. We'll tell them when I'm well into the pregnancy."

"I like that idea. Now, where would you like to go for lunch? Somehow, I don't think I'll be able to get any work done if I go back to the office."

"Me either," Daphne laughed. "How about I pick up something and we can check out these places online?" she added, holding up the brochures.

"Fine with me. I'll see you at the house." Britton headed to her car. She watched a single bird fly across the clear blue sky as she waited for Daphne's Mercedes to back out. A smile crossed her face as Daphne waved cheerfully, driving past her.

~

Both women spent the rest of the afternoon looking bug-eyed at the computer monitor.

"Who knew this would be so difficult?" Daphne sighed.

"It's not like getting a dog. This is some serious shit. We can't pick an idiot or someone who looks better with a bag over his head. How do people do this?" Britton pushed the computer back onto Daphne's lap.

"I have an idea." Daphne set the laptop aside and jumped up, trotting across the house towards Britton's office. She returned a minute later with paper and pencils. "Here, you write down your top five qualities, plus the looks you're looking for. I'll do mine and we'll compare notes. Then, we'll take are similarities and plug them into the questionnaire. This should help us narrow our search."

Britton leaned over, kissing Daphne's temple.

"What was that for?"

"I love you." She grinned.

"I love you too. Now, get to work. If we can't decide on sperm donor qualities, we're going to wind up in a nursing home, letting some stranger bath us and wipe our asses," Daphne joked.

Britton chuckled as she began her list. She wanted someone with a college education and artistic ability. As far as looks, she wished she could make the child look just like Daphne with blonde hair and pretty green eyes, so she wrote those down as her top two qualities. Then, thinking that if it were a boy, she didn't want to have to stand on the dining table to scold him when he'd done something wrong, so she picked a slim build with no one over five foot ten. Happy with her choices, she set her pen and paper down and waited for Daphne.

"That was quick," Daphne uttered.

"I'm easy."

"I know," Daphne teased.

"I resent that remark!" Britton exclaimed, tickling her side.

"Stop, Britton!" she squealed. "I won't be able to finish if you make me pee my damn pants!"

"Gross! Not on the couch!"

"Oh, like we haven't done other things to get stains on this couch!"

"Those are memorable," Britton chided.

"Uh huh." Daphne smiled.

~

Britton went outside to check the mail and give herself something to do. She returned a few minutes later to find Daphne's pencil and paper lying next to hers, but the blonde was nowhere in sight. Britton sat down, looking around quickly before perusing her wife's choices.

"I see you!" Daphne said, from the hallway, causing Britton to scream like a little girl. She laughed hysterically as she sat down next to her. "I caught you cheating."

Mommies

"Oh, please," Britton shoved her playfully. "We have some of the same answers, except you went with brown hair, gray eyes, and six feet tall."

Daphne looked at her paper. "Since it will have my genes, I thought a donor who shared your qualities would be better, so we'd get a mix."

"I'm not six feet tall."

"What if we have a boy? Do you want him to be a dwarf?"

"No," Britton giggled. "But, I don't want him to be so tall that we can't keep him in line either. I went with average height and a slim build."

"That makes sense. It's not really fair to stunt his growth because of disciplinary issues we may or may not have, but I see your point. Plus, if it's a girl, we don't want her to be extremely tall either."

"Exactly. I know nothing about basketball," Britton added.

Daphne put their lists together and began plugging the choices into the survey boxes. A few minutes later, the generated list popped up.

"Fifteen out of two-thousand?" Britton questioned, folding her arms.

"That's because you want a nerd," Daphne smirked.

"No it's not. It's because you want an athlete," she challenged.

"Either way, it's a good thing. We need to get to one, so our chances just got a hell of a lot better."

"How do we narrow it more?"

"Well, these five here are pretty popular. See, they've all had six births."

"Okay, so now we're down to ten."

"We shouldn't decide this all in one day. These guys all have qualities we like and dislike, so let's think on it for a few days and take the time to read about each one. Who knows? We may come up with other things we want to add or take away before making the final decision," Daphne said.

"What about the girls who get drunk in a club and take home the nearest guy? They aren't really thinking about qualities other than physical attributes," Britton added.

"Exactly my point. Have you looked at the news lately? The idiot pool is multiplying."

Britton nodded in agreement. "This really is a lot to think about."

"Besides, Dr. Rooney said we had a couple of weeks."

"Are we going to do it this next cycle?" Britton asked.

"I guess it depends on whether we find a donor, but I don't see why not. Unless you want to wait?"

Britton swallowed nervously. "No. I'm ready when you are."

"I can't believe we're doing this."

"Me neither." Britton smiled. "Who knew life with you would be such an adventure?"

"Me? How about life with you? It's like Mr. Toad's Wild Ride at Disney World!"

"What's that?" Britton asked.

"Haven't you been to Disney World?"

"Yes. I went when I was down there drawing Hogwarts for that college project. I went to all of the parks. I don't remember a toad ride."

"Hmm…maybe it's gone. It was my favorite as a kid."

Britton shrugged.

"Well, I guess we'll see when we take our daughter or son there one day," Daphne said, grabbing and squeezing her hand.

Chapter 7

Britton's dark sports car pulled into the parking lot of the sushi restaurant. She got out, running her hand through her hair, pushing the chestnut locks off her shoulder as she shut the door and scurried inside. It had been three days since she and Daphne had met with the fertility doctor and began their search for a sperm donor. She spent a few hours each day reading and rereading the profiles of the ten men on their list, narrowing her choices down to five, but of the five, she simply couldn't decide which one she wanted to share her child's genes. This decision was proving to be nearly as difficult as getting married had been. As an artist, she hated narrowing choices. She liked having free reign to let her mind flow. "You look lost in thought," Heather said as her best friend slid into the booth seat across from her. "I already ordered since I knew you'd be running late."

Britton smiled and shook her head. "I think the traffic is getting worse downtown."

"Yeah. It's because of our wonderful mayor and his plans to revitalize the streets. I swear, most of my regular routes are under construction."

"Don't get me started on that asshole," Britton growled. "He's an arrogant, homophobic weasel who has done nothing but waste my time."

Heather laughed. "What now?"

"The governor wants to build a new art museum and before the governor had even announced which city it was going to be in, Mayor Ass Napkin had me put some sketches together."

"Let me guess, he hated them."

"No, he had a bunch of other firms around the state do it, too, after telling me he wanted me to design it. So, now I'm in a bidding war with at least four other companies, one of which I used to work for."

"That sucks."

"Exactly. If I'd known he was going to use me to get the governor to choose Providence, I wouldn't have done it in the first place. I thought he'd chosen me as the architect and was simply using my prelim design. When he called me yesterday to tell me there were other designs with lower bids than mine, I wanted to reach through the phone and choke him to death!"

"Sing it girl!" Heather cheered, causing Britton to laugh hysterically.

"Man, he pisses me off," she said, shaking her head.

"So, besides the mayor shitting in your sandbox, what else is going on?"

Britton thought about the five donors and all of the difficulty she'd been having trying to choose between them. *I hate not being able to get your help with this,* she thought as she answered, "Not much of anything. What about you?"

"I hired the painters. They start next week."

"Cool. Did Greg like the colors?"

"He didn't help pick them out, so I don't think he has a choice in the matter. It's all earthy browns and tans with white trim like you suggested."

"I think that'll look great," Britton added.

"Me too. I'll be glad when it's done."

"Hey, I have a question for you, completely off topic. Do you think someone who went to a private college, or a large public university is smarter?"

"I don't know. I went to community college. Why?"

"Kathleen asked me."

Heather nodded.

"You're in the medical field. If someone's grandfather had diabetes, what are the chances of that person getting it, if no one else has it?"

"What the hell? These sound like word questions on the SAT test. I don't know. I'm a dental hygienist, not a doctor." Heather took a sip from her water glass. "What's going on with her?"

"You know Kathleen's weird. She's good at her job, that's why she's my assistant, but other than that, the woman is out there. I think she's studying for Jeopardy or something."

Heather gave her a strange look and sat back as their food was placed in the center of the table.

"What's it like wearing glasses?" Britton asked.

"I wear contacts."

"I know, but your whole family wears glasses. Is there anyone who doesn't?"

Heather thought for a second. "My dad doesn't. Well, he didn't until he got older. He uses reading glasses for small print, but my mother and I have both worn them all of our lives. Why, do you need glasses?"

"No. Bridget was talking about them. Neither of our parents wear glasses, so I'm not sure what she was talking about."

"Speaking of your sister, what's going with her and Wade? Did you figure that all out?"

"She says they're fine and just doing the career thing right now. She's supposed to talk with our mother, but I don't think that's happened."

"How are you and Daphne?"

"Still in the honeymoon phase," Britton teased.

"I don't want the details," Heather laughed.

Britton had just finished her lunch when her cell phone rang. She looked at the caller ID and lit up when she saw Daphne's face.

"Go talk to your wife and tell her I said hey," Heather said.

"I love you. We'll plan a wine night soon," Britton replied, tossing some cash on the table and hugging best friend.

"Who are you loving and having wine with?" Daphne asked.

"Your cousin," Britton answered. "She says hi, by the way."

"Have you worked on your list?"

"Yes." Britton waited for the Bluetooth in her car to pick up the call, before driving off. "I narrowed it to five."

"Well, we should probably narrow it a little more. My period started today. We need to get the donor name to the doctor's office so they can order it. Ovulation should start in ten to fourteen days."

"Wow. Okay." Britton missed a gear as she shifted. Her mind was going a hundred miles an hour. "I guess we'll compare notes tonight."

"Sounds good. I'll see you soon!"

Britton loved hearing the excitement in Daphne's voice. "I love you," she said before ending the call.

~

Kathleen had left a note on Britton's desk to call the mayor, which she found when she walked in from lunch. She wasn't in the mood to talk to him, so she tossed it aside and went to her drawing desk.

"Did you get my message?" Kathleen asked a little while later.

"Yes. What does he want now?"

"He wants to set up a meeting to go over your bid. He also mentioned something about the sketches needing some changes."

"Asshole," Britton muttered.

Kathleen laughed and turned to leave the room.

"Hey, Kathleen, do you think someone's astrological sign or favorite subject in school are important?"

"Stay away from Pisces, they'll make you crazy. Other than that, neither," she said, walking away.

Britton raised her eyebrows in surprise. "I'm a Pisces and I'm not crazy," she said to herself. Her mind was going in so many different directions she could barely concentrate.

~

Later that day, Britton couldn't wait to get home. She went into the house, shedding her jacket as she walked through the kitchen. She furrowed her brow as she looked around for her wife. "Daph?" she called out.

"In here, babe!" Daphne yelled from the den.

Britton stepped out of her dress shoes, leaving them in the dining room as she made her way towards the back of the house.

Daphne was sitting on the couch, wearing an old pair of cotton shorts and a t-shirt, and surrounded by papers. She lifted her eyes when she felt a presence in the room. Britton was standing a few feet away, dressed in her sleeveless crème colored blouse and dark gray slacks. Daphne moved some of the pages and patted the cushion next to her.

"You look busy," Britton said, sitting down and leaning over to kiss her softly. "How long have you been home?"

Daphne shrugged. "I left early to get a head start. I couldn't concentrate on anything in the office."

Britton bit her lower lip and nodded.

"I've looked at everything on these five men so many times, my head is spinning. I like certain things about each one, but I find faults in all of them as well. Have you gotten any further?" Daphne asked.

Britton moved to the side and pulled Daphne back against her chest. "We all have faults. That's part of being human," she said, kissing the side of Daphne's head. "Are there things I wish I could change about each one, sure, but will it really be a big deal if he or she wears glasses or is a Virgo? I mean, we can change some of the variables like what type of college he or she goes to. We are both physically active, healthy people. I'm sure we'll instill those values in our child as well. I just don't see why we're beating ourselves up over variables that we can't change." She wrapped her arms a little tighter around Daphne.

"You're right," Daphne sighed. "This should be exciting, not nerve-racking. Maybe I am thinking too much."

"I love you and this is the biggest decision of our lives, so it shouldn't exactly be a cakewalk, but I've stared at those papers for hours and it's impossible to decide one over the other. If I had to choose right now, I'd say number 14268. He fits all of the physical characteristics that we want; he has a master's degree; his hobbies are: jogging, hiking, reading books, painting with water colors, and traveling. Who cares if he wears glasses and his grandfather, who died from a stroke, was from France?"

Daphne giggled. "He sounds gay."

"So are you!" Britton laughed.

Daphne sat up and turned, pressing her lips to Britton's. "I love you," she murmured, pulling away slightly. "Number 14268 it is."

"Are you sure?" Britton questioned.

"Yes." She smiled. "I agree. He fits what we are looking for."

"What if the kid turns out gay?"

"So are you!" Daphne exclaimed with a grin.

Britton watched her get up and walk away. "Where are you going?" she asked.

"To call the doctor's office. Even if they don't answer, I can leave a message for them to hear first thing in the morning." Daphne was nearly bouncing with giddiness as she left the room.

Britton inhaled deeply and let her breath out slowly before getting up to go change her clothes and peruse the takeout menus, knowing Daphne would want to celebrate their latest accomplishment.

Chapter 8

Britton had just hung up with the mayor after agreeing to meet him later that morning when Daphne's face appeared on her ringing cell phone. She quickly answered the call.

"Leave the morning of the fourteenth open on your calendar," Daphne said with a shaky voice. "Actually, you might want to leave that Monday and Wednesday as well."

"What's going on?"

"We're being inseminated!" Daphne exclaimed with excitement.

"Already? We just picked the donor. Don't they need to do things? Run tests?" Britton questioned nervously.

"No. We're all set. A few days after Aunt Flow leaves, I have to start peeing on those ovulation stick things. She went ahead and tentatively scheduled it for the fourteenth, but it could actually be anytime that week she said."

"Okay, so what happens with the stick?"

"As soon as we get the smiley face I have to call her office. They'll inseminate that day."

Holy shit, this is happening, Britton thought, taking a deep breath. "Wow. I guess I thought we wouldn't make this cycle."

"Yeah, I was a little surprised too," Daphne admitted.

"Wish I could kiss you right now," Britton murmured.

"I wish I could do a lot more than that," Daphne added.

"My schedule is wide open today. Want to meet for lunch?" Britton teased.

Daphne giggled. "We're married and live together. I don't think we have to sneak around to have sex anymore."

"Who said we'd be sneaking? I'd tell Kathleen I'm going to go get it on with my wife, and I'll be back in a couple of hours."

"Oh, God," Daphne laughed hysterically. "Aunt Flow is here, remember? Go back to work. I just wanted to let you know so you could clear your schedule. I'll see you tonight. I love you."

"I love you too." Britton ended the call and prepared to meet with the mayor.

~

Britton wasn't thrilled to be dealing with the mayor again, but her business could definitely use the deal for the art museum. She'd thought she was rid of him, until he ran for election in Providence and was voted in.

If the people of this city really knew what you were like... she thought, shaking her head as he sat across from her, going on and on about the changes he wanted her to make to the original sketches.

"Can I ask why you'd like me to incorporate all of these adjustments when we're still in the bidding stage? Has Phil Mason's firm submitted any sketches?" she asked.

"Well…" he fumbled, shuffling papers on his desk.

"I'm not at liberty to discuss each bid."

Britton watched his beady little eyes bounce around as she started to realize what the weasel in front of her was up to. She glared at him in disgust, sitting up straighter in her chair.

"As an avid supporter of the arts, I appreciate the opportunity to bid on the building, but I'm not going to give you sketch after sketch so that you can take them to each business and see if they can produce the same design for less money. I am a professional and I refuse to do business this way. If you want to work with me and my company, you have the sketches, you have my bid, and you know my work." She stood, reaching for her briefcase as she prepared to leave.

"Wait," he said, holding his hand up.

Britton raised an eyebrow and crossed her arms.

"If you can make the changes I suggested and come within ten percent of Phil Mason's bid, the job is yours," he sighed.

"He can't do it, can he?"

"His design isn't modern enough, and he was unable to recreate your original lines."

She grinned. "Let me get back to the office, look at my original bid, and update the sketches. I'll have an answer for you before the end of the day."

As she walked out of City Hall, she looked up at the cloudless sky and felt the sun's rays warming her cheeks. Standing up to that righteous piece of shit made her feel ten feet tall. She smiled brightly and added a little pep to her step as she walked to her car.

~

The rest of Britton's day went by in a flash. She worked through lunch improving the sketches for the museum, then spent the next two hours reworking her bid, until she was able to finally make it meet the mayor's new parameters.

After the courier left with the latest bid and sketches, Britton flopped down into her desk chair and let out a deep sigh as she flung her head back. Working with deadlines and finicky people was nothing new to her. Being an architect, she encountered those on a weekly basis from client to client. No, it was the impeding insemination that was weighing on the back of her mind. She wanted a family with Daphne, and she had no reservations about what they were doing, but she hadn't paid much attention to the time frames as Dr. Rooney went over everything. Instead, she was caught up in the technical and physicality's of the procedure itself. So, she had been caught completely off guard when Daphne called that morning to give her the exact date…only ten days away.

She tried to imagine what she'd be doing in nine months. If everything went through with the mayor and they started right away, the art museum could possibly be built by then and scheduling a grand opening. She also had a number of other bids coming up that she was actively working on, including the English Cottage for

Senator Ferguson, who was still twiddling his thumbs on the location for the build.

The last few minutes before five p.m. ticked by slowly on her wall clock.

"It's quitting time," Kathleen said from the doorway, startling Britton. "You look like you're somewhere else. Vacation maybe?"

"I wish," Britton laughed.

"I'm headed out. Are you staying late?"

"No. I'm right behind you," Britton replied, grabbing her briefcase.

They walked across the small parking lot together. As soon as Britton was in her car, she dialed Heather's number.

"Hey, you!" Heather answered.

"How's the painting going?"

"They finished yesterday. Greg and I were up most of the night putting the house back together."

"How does it look?"

"Like we live in the great plains or something," she laughed. "I love it! The neutral colors actually make the house look bigger."

"That's always a plus."

"Yep, so what's new with you and Daphne?"

"Nothing much. We've both been busy with work, which is why I'm calling. Are you doing anything this weekend?"

"No. Not that I know of."

"We should do a wine night. We haven't had one in a while."

"Yeah, I agree. Who knew getting married would slow down the almighty Britton Prescott?" she teased.

"Oh, please. You did a lot more when you were single too."

"Uh huh, but we did twice as much when you were single!" she replied. "Anyway, I'm free. Let me know what day, and my house or yours?"

"Doesn't matter. I'll see what Daphne has planned. She mentioned doing something with Bridget Friday after work, I think."

"Okay. Hey, next time you're schmoozing with the mayor, ask him what the hell plans on doing with this gridlock traffic downtown. I swear things have gotten worse in the city since he was elected."

"Don't get me started on that pencil dick. I didn't vote for him!"

"Me either!"

Britton heard a horn honking on the phone. "I better let you go. It sounds like you're in a mess."

"You're not in this? What did you do, leave early?"

"No. I go the opposite way, remember?"

"I forgot you don't have to backtrack through town. I should've been smart and bought a house outside of Providence too."

"Yep. Be careful. I'll call you tomorrow about Friday," Britton said, before hanging up.

Chapter 9

Daphne was hanging their dry-cleaning when Britton walked into the bedroom, wrapping her arms around her wife's mid-section and kissing the side of her neck.

"What was that for?" Daphne purred, turning in Britton's arms to kiss her tenderly.

"I missed you and I love you."

Daphne pursed her lips teasingly in thought, and then smiled brightly. "I love you, too. How was your day?"

"I told the mayor off."

"No, you didn't."

"Yes I did. Right in his office as a matter of fact," Britton said, as she pulled away to take off her work clothes.

"Wow. And I thought I went a little over the edge today," Daphne replied shaking her head.

"What did you do?" Britton stopped what she was doing and turned to face her, dressed only in dark slacks and a satin bra.

"I drank a glass of wine at lunch." Daphne shook her head. "I needed to calm my nerves."

Britton laughed. "Seriously? Heather and I used to have a drink at lunch all the time and go back to work."

Daphne rolled her eyes. "That doesn't surprise me. The two of you don't exactly follow the rules." She grinned.

Britton hung her pants and pulled an old pair of shorts and a tank top before pulling Daphne back into her arms. "That's why you've been in love with me for so many years. I don't walk the line."

"Uh huh," Daphne giggled and kissed her. "So, what did the mayor do now?"

"If I could bitch slap him and get away with it, I would've done it months ago!" she fumed. "That weasel tried to play Phil Mason against me and lost when Phil couldn't mimic the design I gave him."

"What an asshole."

"Exactly. I told him straight up, this is how it is, take it or leave it."

"What did he do?" Daphne asked as Britton backed away and walked out of the closet into their bedroom.

"As of the voicemail I got when I pulled into the driveway, he took it. The signed contract should be on my desk by morning."

"Way to go, babe!" Daphne exclaimed, smacking her butt.

Britton spun around. "Did you just slap my ass?"

Daphne bit her lower lip and shrugged as her face began to turn pink. Britton laughed and pushed her back onto the bed, climbing on top of her.

"Are we football players now?" Britton teased.

"I have no idea where that came from. Your butt looks great in those shorts. I couldn't help it."

"I see." Britton bent down, claiming her lips in a heated kiss as she moved against her.

Daphne pulled away breathless. "As much as I want you right now, I'm not going there."

Britton looked at her with a questioning expression.

"Aunt Flow!"

"Oh, yeah. I forgot about that," Britton huffed, rolling to the side.

"I don't understand why you never get yours at the same time. Most women who are around each other often, share the same cycle."

Britton shrugged. "I'd be happy if it never came again. As far as I'm concerned, that old bitch can move out and stay out."

Daphne pushed against her playfully.

"How many more days until it's gone? I think I have blue clit," Britton pouted.

Daphne laughed hysterically. "That's not a thing."

"Yes it is. Want to see?" she joked.

"No." Daphne shook her head, still chuckling as she sat up and walked out of the room.

"What's for dinner?" Britton called out.

"Duck!" Daphne yelled back.

"Duck?" Britton murmured, getting off the bed to go investigate.

Daphne was near the stove, pulling pans from the cabinet when Britton stepped into the room. She leaned back against the wall, watching her wife bending over.

"I see you," Daphne said.

Britton turned around and bent over, looking through her legs at Daphne. "I see you too, and I am not eating duck for dinner."

Daphne guffawed as she stood up. "You're a mess, you know that?"

"I thought I was trouble," Britton retorted, standing up and taking a seat on a stool next to the island in the center of the kitchen.

"You're that too," she said, opening the refrigerator.

"Why would you want to eat a duck? You love feeding them and watching them swim in the bay."

Daphne shook her head as she pulled the ingredients out of the fridge for their dinner and closed the door. "I was razzing you for questioning me about dinner."

Britton smiled as she watched her. "Would you like a glass of wine? Or did you drink too much at lunch?"

"Very funny, smartass." Daphne tried not to smile. "A glass of wine would be nice. Thank you."

Britton walked into the dining room to get a bottle from the wine cooler. "Speaking of wine, do you still have plans with Bridget this weekend?" she asked, walking back into the kitchen.

"Yes. We're having dinner Friday night after work. Why? Do you want to meet us?"

"No. I'm going over to Heather's, but I wanted to make sure I had the night right." Britton opened the bottle and poured two glasses of chardonnay.

Daphne nodded, picking up one of the glasses. "I'm going to miss this."

"Wine?"

"Yes. You can't drink when you're pregnant."

"That's a deal breaker for me, for sure." Britton shook her head.

"A lot of things are deal breakers for you," Daphne snickered. "I think Hell would freeze over before you carried a baby for nine months."

"You got that right. You're on your own with the baby oven."

"Do you plan on being in the room when the doctor does the procedure?" Daphne teased.

"I'm not letting you out of my sight," Britton said seriously.

"Okay, just checking."

Britton set her wine glass down. "Daphne, you're my entire world. I'm going to be right beside you every step of the way, no matter what. We're in this together."

Daphne walked over, wrapping her arms around Britton's neck. "I love you so damn much."

Britton grinned and kissed her tenderly, lingering before pushing the kiss deeper.

Daphne pulled away. "Don't start something we can't finish."

"We can…but…"

"Yeah, no thanks."

"Good! I agree!" Britton grimaced.

Chapter 10

Britton ran her hand through her wavy locks, pushing them back over her shoulder as she waited for Heather to open the door.

"Sorry. I was on the phone and didn't hear the knocking," Heather said as she pulled the door open and hugged her best friend.

"Everything okay?"

"Yeah. You know my mom will talk your ears off if you let her. You'd think we lived in different states, instead of fifteen minutes apart."

"Want to trade?" Britton chided with a smile.

"My favorite lesbian!" Greg exclaimed, hearing her voice as he walked out of the bedroom. He wrapped his arm around her shoulder's. "How's that wife of yours?"

"Unbelievable!" she teased with a wink.

"Are you sure you never had any lesbian tendencies?" he asked Heather, having the same fantasy as most men about being with two women.

"Well, there was that one time she got a little drunk and we—"

"Oh, don't egg him on with lies. He already has a crush on you," Heather laughed.

Greg rolled his eyes and walked over to Heather, kissing her softly. "I'll be back around eleven."

"Have fun," she said.

"Where are you headed?" Britton asked.

"It's poker night. Want to go?"

"I thought it was guys only."

"We'll make an exception for you." He smiled.

Britton grinned. "I wouldn't mind taking easy money from a bunch of boys, but I have a date with your wife."

"Don't do anything with her that I would do," he joked as he walked out the door.

"I love him," Britton laughed.

"Me too." Heather smiled. "So, I wasn't sure if you were in the mood for red or white, so I got both."

"Sounds great."

"Long week?" Heather asked, walking into the kitchen.

"You have no idea." Britton leaned against the counter, watching her open the bottle of merlot. When both glasses were poured, she grabbed hers, swooshing it around before holding it up.

"Cheers to…a great weekend?" Heather shrugged.

"Fine with me." Britton touched her glass to Heather's and took a long swallow, enjoying the taste as it coated her throat. "Could you imagine going nine months without this?" she murmured.

"Why? Are you pregnant?" Heather raised an eyebrow.

"Hell no. Have we met?" Britton shook her head.

Heather laughed. "Well, where did that come from?"

"Kathleen was talking about all the things she gave up when she was pregnant. I think she's freaking out because her only child is about to go away to college."

"Oh." Heather nodded. "How's work going?"

"Good. The Hardy Sporting Goods building is getting inspected next week, and I got the deal for the new art museum after I told the mayor off."

"What?" Heather giggled. "I'm surprised you're working with him again at all."

"I know. He's a dick, but it's a great opportunity and my design is unlike anything I've ever created. It's definitely going to stand out."

"Do you think he's going to be a pain in the ass the entire time?"

"I have no idea. He's was just a pervert the last time we worked together. Now that his true colors have come out, who knows?" She took a sip from her glass. "If he does, I'll make sure he's buried under the foundation." She beamed.

"The city will thank you!" Heather chuckled.

"What about you? How's the dental office?"

"Same routine, different teeth." She shrugged. "We do have a new dentist. That's been the only exciting thing lately. The other hygienists have been a little catty because of it."

"Is he an ass?"

"Actually, *she* is really nice and very young. I think they're jealous of her or something."

"Is she hot?"

Heather raised an eyebrow.

"I don't mean for me." Britton shook her head.

"You know, when I first met her, I thought of you. She's the type you would've made an appointment with, despite the fact that you hate the dentist."

"My dog days are long over," Britton laughed. "Nothing will ever come between me and Daphne, she said seriously.

"Oh, I know that. It's obvious. Anyway, Dr. Milner is pretty: dirty blond hair, blue eyes, slim figure, and she's barely out of medical school. You know Dr. Wilcox treats all of the women in the office like they're all his. I guess they think Dr. Milner is going to steal him away, when he's none of theirs to begin with."

"Straight women," Britton muttered, shaking her head as she refilled their glasses.

"Hey, don't add me into that mix. I've never found that dirty old man attractive. I think that's why we get along so well. I give him hell and call him out on it when he flirts with me."

"I wonder if he knows the mayor..." Britton laughed.

"Who knows? So, what do you and Daphne have planned for the weekend?"

"Nothing, which is fine with me."

"We're going to a family barbeque tomorrow for Greg's company," Heather added.

"Dad does those every year, too. I'm always invited, but I never go."

"What about now, since you're married to an employee?"

"I was supposed to go with her last year, but I had an unveiling that same day. She was already home by the time I'd finished. However, this year's picnic is coming up and we're definitely going."

"Is it weird being around his employees?"

"No. I couldn't give a shit what anyone thinks of me. You know that. But, Daphne had a hard time at first.

She didn't want people to think she was being treated any differently because the owner is her father-in-law. They all know she's married to the black sheep." Britton smirked and sipped her wine. "At the office, Daphne operates by the book. She never cuts corners and always acts very professional. Honestly, I think they were blown away to find out she was gay. Then, when she married the owner's wild-child daughter, they were floored."

"Yeah, who would've thought you two would wind up together?" Heather shook her head and smiled. "But, I've never seen either of you happier."

"Thanks. Not to sound cliché, but she really does complete me. I love her with all of my heart and would do anything in the world for her. I've never felt like that about anyone in my life."

"That's because you belong together. I know what's it's like to be two totally different people, but fit so perfectly together. Look at me and Greg. I'm cool, calm, and collected, and he acts like his hair is on fire sometimes. I can't explain it, it just works." She finished the last of her wine and set the glass in the sink. "Speaking of marriages, what's going on with your sister? Is your mom still hounding her about having kids?"

"I have no idea. Bridget and Wade are fine and don't want kids right now. I'm not getting involved any further because if I do, my mom will turn all of that on me."

"I can see Daphne as a mom, but do you want kids?"

"Why does everyone think I don't?"

"Because for years you hated the idea of marriage and babies," Heather said, crossing her arms as she leaned back against the counter.

"A lot has changed. I guess I've grown up." Britton shrugged. "I want a family with Daphne, but we agreed that it will be our terms and no one else's, if and when the time comes. What about you?"

"You know I want kids, just not any time soon. Greg and I are happy with the way things are and we're nowhere near ready for that step."

Britton noticed the time on the stove clock. "I should probably get home. If I drink anymore, I'll become a house guest."

Heather laughed. "Wouldn't be the first time for either of us."

Britton hugged her. "I'll call you this week, maybe we can do lunch. I have a lot going on over the next few weeks, so my schedule will be hectic."

Chapter 11

Britton put the top down on her car before she backed out of Heather's driveway. The warm, summer sky was full of stars. A light breeze swirled around her as she drove down the street. There was barely any traffic, making her thirteen-mile drive from Providence to Warwick quicker than usual.

She smiled when she noticed Daphne's black Mercedes parked inside the garage as the door went up. She pulled her Porsche in next to it, and quietly entered the house. She placed her keys on the hook in the kitchen and set her briefcase in her home office before padding softly up the stairs.

The moonlight coming off the bay cast a soft glow across the bedroom. Britton felt her chest ache when her eyes landed on the lump on the right side of the large bed. She stepped into the closet, replacing her blouse with a thin tank top and tossing her slacks into the dry-cleaning pile on the floor. She finished getting ready for bed and slid in-between the covers.

"I'm awake," Daphne murmured groggily as she curled up against her.

Britton kissed Daphne's cheek. She was sound asleep before Britton could ask about her evening.

~

The next morning, Britton pried her eyes open, checking to see if it was still dark outside so she could sleep a little longer.

"Hi," Daphne whispered.

Britton looked into the light green eyes staring back at her. "Were you watching me sleep?"

Daphne smiled sheepishly. "When you wake up next to a beautiful woman, it's hard not to look at her."

Britton moved closer, pressing her lips to Daphne's in a gentle kiss that quickly heated up as Daphne rolled to her back, pulling Britton with her. Feeling Daphne's hips moving against hers, Britton broke the kiss.

"What about—"

"It's gone." Daphne grinned.

"Really? It's only been three days."

"You know I have short periods."

"Aren't you little miss perfect period," she teased.

"Are we seriously still talking about this?" Daphne asked, pushing her hips up into the woman on top of her.

Britton bit her bottom lip before going in for another passionate kiss. She ran her hand slowly down Daphne's side, sliding it under the thin shirt she was wearing, caressing her breasts as she kissed her.

Daphne pushed Britton's tank top up, breaking the kiss as she pulled the shirt over her head, and tossed it to the floor. Britton sat back, removing Daphne's shirt as well, before leaning down, teasing Daphne's lips with her tongue, pulling away and making Daphne chase her each time she tried to press their lips together.

Impatient with the come-hither, playful banter, Daphne rolled Britton to her back, kissing her hard before sliding down her body. Britton's black, bikini panties were removed and flung to the floor as Daphne traced her tongue up Britton's inner thigh and back down the other side without touching her sweet spot. When Britton's thighs began to tremble, Daphne dipped her head, licking softly between the wet folds.

Britton's heart raced and her chest heaved. She fought to get control of her body as Daphne's mouth sent her to another level. She grasped the sheets and squeezed her eyes closed, desperately trying to hold on as Daphne's tongue moved delicately, barely brushing the edges of her throbbing center. She bucked her hips, trying to increase the pressure, but Daphne only backed away, slowing her mouth even further.

Daphne watched Britton writhe under her liked a caged animal as she controlled her lover's release. Deciding she'd kept her on the edge long enough, Daphne shifted her mouth, driving long, hard strokes over her center.

Britton cried out, gasping for breath. She felt like she was soaring through the universe as wave after wave of pleasure washed over her. When her heart rate came back to a somewhat normal pace, her eyes flickered open. Daphne's head was resting on her thigh and pale green eyes were staring back at her.

"Who are you and what have you done with my wife?" Britton croaked, still trying to gather herself.

"I thought you liked teasing." Daphne grinned, crawling back up.

"Uh huh," Britton murmured, shaking her head. "Come here," she added with a smile.

Mommies

Daphne curled into her arms, kissing her tenderly.

Tasting herself on Daphne's mouth turned the smoldering embers of Britton's libido back into a raging fire. She pushed Daphne to her back and moved over her. Daphne's hips rose as Britton's hand slid lower, parting her soaked folds with precise strokes before slipping easily inside.

Daphne wrapped her arms around Britton, running her hands up and down her back.

"I see you enjoyed your little game," Britton whispered, pushing deeper as she kissed her hard.

Daphne moved her hips with the same rhythm as Britton's fingers, matching her thrust for thrust. She was already close from watching Britton's body react to her touches, so it didn't take long for her to reach the edge. She dug her short nails into Britton's back and broke the kiss, gasping as she tried to hold on a little longer.

Britton rubbed her thumb over Daphne's clit, causing her to tremble with release. Britton stilled her hand, feeling Daphne tighten around her fingers, over and over. "I love you," she whispered, kissing Daphne's cheek.

"I love you, too," Daphne murmured breathlessly.

Britton slowly pulled her fingers free, rubbing them along Daphne's inner thigh. The cool air chilled their sweaty skin as Britton moved off of her, settling at her side.

Daphne turned her head, looking into the gray eyes gazing back at her. Then she reached up, pushing Britton's hair over her shoulder before kissing her lips softly. "What are we going to do today?" she asked.

"We're already doing it," Britton replied.

Daphne laughed. "I love you, but you're on your own, babe. I'm not staying in bed all day."

"Do you remember what life was like before we got married?" Britton asked.

"Of course. We never saw each other, so we had a reason to spend the weekend in bed. Now, I see you every day and sleep next to you every night." Daphne kissed her again before getting out of the bed.

Britton watched her naked wife walk across the room. She got up and headed downstairs to start a pot of coffee when she heard the shower start. A blue light was blinking on her cell phone, indicating she had a voicemail.

Britton, it's your mother. Have you and Daphne had a chance to talk with Bridget? I left her a message asking if she needed our family attorney's information, but she hasn't returned my call.. Anyway, give me a call when you get this. Love you.

Britton rolled her eyes and set the phone down. Her mother was nothing, if not persistent. She wondered why Bridget hadn't talked to her like she said she was going to do. The aroma of coffee began to fill the air, livening Britton's senses. She pulled a mug out of the cabinet, grabbed the flavored creamer from the fridge, and opened the sugar canister, as she waited in anticipation for the machine to stop.

As soon as the last drop fell into the pot, Britton poured herself a generous cup and went to work adding in the cream and sugar to make it consumable. After a few long sips, she grabbed the phone and pushed the button to call her mother. She didn't feel like talking to her, but if she didn't return the call, she'd never hear the end of it.

"Hello, darling. Did you get my message?" Sharon Prescott asked.

"Yes," Britton sighed. "Mom, Bridget and Wade are fine. She told me so herself."

"Then, why is she avoiding me? I understand that coming from you because you go through life like your hair is on fire, but your sister is like me. She's grounded and methodical."

"I don't know. I told her to call you. I guess I can tell her again," she said, taking another long sip.

"I'll wait for her call then."

"That's a great idea," Britton replied, seeing Daphne appear out of the corner of her eye, freshly showered.

"What are you and Daphne doing today? I will be in the area this afternoon and was thinking of stopping by."

Britton held her finger to her lips when Daphne's eyes met hers. "She's gone off with her mother to shop for plants and I'm working on a model for a client."

"Plants?" Daphne mouthed.

Britton shot her look.

"All right, well, Daddy says hello."

"Tell him we…I mean I said hi."

"Maybe we can do Sunday brunch next week, all of us."

"I'll call Bridget and get back to you."

"Sounds good. Love you, dear."

"Love you too, Mom."

Britton set the phone down and drank another long swallow of coffee.

"You're going to hell for lying to your mother," Daphne chided.

Graysen Morgen

"Oh, please. That woman drives me crazy."

"She's your mother, Britton. How would you feel if our son or daughter avoided us and told us lies to keep us away?"

Britton sighed. "I'd hate it."

"Well, be a little nicer to her then or karma will come back around on you."

"She sent Bridget our family attorney's info in case she's filing for divorce."

"Are you serious?" Daphne gasped, nearly spewing coffee.

"Yep. She's not so innocent is she?"

Daphne pursed her lips. "I told Bridget to talk to her."

"I have no idea why she's so scared of our mother. She's always been that way. Like it's the end of the world if she disapproves of something." Britton shook her head.

"You're that way with your father," Daphne added.

"True, but that's because he spent my college years being so disappointed in me for not doing what he wanted me to do, that he missed out on all of the good that I was doing for myself. We're past that now, finally."

"Your parents are both different, that's for sure, but they love you and your sister and only do what they think is right. I'll talk to Bridget again, but you need to stop alienating your mother. When we have a child, she's going to be around all of the time." Daphne gave her a stern look.

"I know that."

"Besides, I think they've both figured out by now that they can't run your life. Britton Prescott does

72

whatever she wants, whenever she wants, and however she wants."

"Exactly." Britton grinned. "And speaking of doing—"

Daphne moved closer, kissing her lips. "Not happening," she laughed softly as she pulled away.

"There goes my perfect weekend," Britton sighed.

Chapter 12

The following week, Britton walked into the exam room behind Daphne. She was a little nervous, unsure what to expect as she watched Daphne change into the paper gown and climb up on the table.

"Here we go," Daphne said with a nervous smile.

"Piece of cake," Britton replied, squeezing her hand and kissing her cheek.

"Hello, ladies!" Dr. Rooney bounced into the room like a ball of energy. "Are we ready to make a baby?"

"Yep," Daphne replied.

"Hot damn, let's get started!" Dr. Rooney clapped her hands together. "Go ahead and lie back and let's do a quick ultrasound to see exactly where you are with the ovulation process."

Britton held her wife's hand while she watched the doctor run the small camera receiver over Daphne's abdomen and study the black and white blob on the screen.

She typed a few notes and backed away from the screen. "It looks like you're in mid-ovulation," she said reaching for something that looked like a toothpaste tube with a long, slender tip. "When you ovulate, your body produces a thick, fertile fluid called cervical mucus. It lubricates everything and cradles the sperm, allowing it to swim freely to its destination. Some women don't produce enough of this natural mucus, causing the sperm to die before they ever have a chance to swim upstream. This is an artificial lubricant that works the same way. I'm going to squirt a little inside to help coat everything and up our chances," she added. "It's going to feel a little cold, but your body heat will warm it up quickly. Go ahead and slide to the end of the table and put your feet in the stirrups."

Daphne nodded and Britton turned her head, not wanting to watch the doctor insert the lubricant.

"All right. It usually takes a few minutes for the liquid to work its way inside. Stay flat on your back and try not to move. I'll be back with your little swimmers in just a couple of minutes." Dr. Rooney smiled, pushing away from the table and tossing her gloves in the trash on her way out.

"Is it me, or does she seem to enjoy this a little too much?" Britton murmured.

Daphne laughed. "She's definitely different, but I like the fact that she's straightforward. This process isn't the easiest thing to go through, so I'm glad it's not stale and calculated. I like her."

Britton shrugged. "Does that stuff feel weird?"

"It's a little cold, but other than that, I just feel extremely wet."

"I don't think you've ever had a problem with that." Britton grinned.

Daphne playfully smacked her arm.

A couple minutes later, Dr. Rooney waltzed back into the room, but this time her nurse followed her. "Okay, here they are. Say hello to the other half of your baby's DNA," she exclaimed, holding up a syringe with a long, thin tube coming from the end of it.

Britton raised her eyebrows and Daphne choked back a laugh.

The nurse ran the ultrasound camera across Daphne's flat stomach as Dr. Rooney moved between her legs.

"Here we go!" she cheered as she inserted the syringe between Daphne's legs and slowly released the vial full of sperm.

Everyone watched the screen as the liquid spread.

"Is that it?" Britton asked, feeling like she might lose her lunch.

"Yep. That's about a million little sperm swimming along. They're microscopic, but that fluid you see moving all around the uterus is full of them."

"Great." Britton nodded.

Daphne squeezed her hand and Britton looked over, seeing tears in her eyes.

"All done, ladies." Dr. Rooney patted both of their shoulders. "Lie still for about ten minutes, then you're free to leave. I suggest no vigorous activity like going to the gym or anything like that."

"Thank you so much," Daphne replied, shaking her hand.

"You're welcome. Don't take a pregnancy test until your period is at least three days late. At that point, you should see a clear positive and be able to call us with the result. Obviously, if you start menstruating, it didn't take. You'll need to let us know that as well. Don't get discouraged, sometimes these things take a few tries. I'll see you both soon."

Britton pulled the stool up near the exam table and sat back down.

"I love you," Daphne said, brushing the hair from Britton's brow.

"I love you, too." Britton leaned over, kissing her softly. "We did it."

"Yeah. Pretty crazy, huh?" Daphne blew out a deep breath.

"Uh huh." Britton nodded. "Are you going back to the office?"

"I thought about going home, but I should be fine at the office. I have over a dozen sick days, but I'm sure I'll need them during the pregnancy."

"That's true. I guess sitting at a desk is fine."

"She only said no gym. I think I'll be okay."

Britton eyed the clock on the wall. "Your ten minutes are up."

"Good. I feel yucky," Daphne grimaced, sitting up to wipe the excess lubricant off herself.

"Yucky?" Britton laughed.

"Yes. Some of that stuff she squirted up inside me ran back out."

"Oh, gross." Britton scrunched her face. "This is such a romantic process."

"No kidding." Daphne shook her head.

"Are you hungry?" Britton asked, wrapping her arms around Daphne's waist.

"Not really. I hate to pass on a lunch date with you, though," Daphne replied, threading her arms around Britton's neck.

"It's fine. I'll pick up dinner on the way home and we can curl up on the couch."

"That sounds like a wonderful idea."

"It's a date, Mrs. Prescott." Britton winked.

~

Britton was a nervous wreck for the rest of the week. She hated waiting games, and this was by far the worst one that she'd been a part of. The Hardy Sporting Goods building was set for its final inspection the first of next week, which gave her something to concentrate on. Once the inspector signed off, she was free and clear of that contract and able to spend all of her time and energy on the art museum. The mayor was still going around and around with the city council, arguing over the location, so the project was on hold at the moment.

"Do you think it's too early to look at nursery stuff?" Daphne asked when Britton walked up to her. She was sitting out back, watching the ducks swim in the bay and relaxing under the warm afternoon sun.

"I don't know. Maybe we should wait until it's official," Britton murmured, easing up behind her and wrapping her arms around Daphne's shoulders.

"Yeah, you're probably right. I hate waiting."

"Me too. How are you feeling?"

"I'm fine." Daphne tilted her head back, looking upside down at her wife. "You've been asking me that at least three times a day for the past four days."

"Sorry," Britton sighed. "Maybe we should do something to take our minds off of everything."

"Like what?"

Britton pursed her lips in thought. "The rodeo is in town."

Daphne laughed hysterically. "No thanks. I'd rather watch paint dry."

"Oh! Paint!" Britton lit up like a light bulb went off between her ears. "One of those drink wine and paint a picture places just opened a couple of weeks ago. What about that?"

"I probably shouldn't drink, just in case, besides, I hardly doubt you'd like someone telling you how to paint a picture."

"True." Britton looked out at the water. She knew why Daphne always ventured outside to clear her head. She'd always found the water relaxing too. "If I had a skull right now, I think I'd row until I couldn't lift my arms," Britton said, moving around to sit next to her on the cushioned bench seat.

"Yeah, me too," Daphne replied, curling into her. "I used to be so nuts over you, I'd row for miles and miles, and you were still better than me! That made me downright crazy."

Britton chuckled. "No wonder you made my life hell."

"Those were the good ole days." Daphne grinned.

"For you, maybe. I wouldn't go back to high school if you had a gun to my head. I'd pull the damn trigger for you."

"It wasn't so bad."

Britton shot her serious look. "You were a major bitch. I much prefer you like this," she said, nuzzling her neck and kissing the soft spot below her ear.

"You keep that up and we're going to scare the ducks away."

Britton shrugged as she pulled Daphne into her lap and ran her hand under Daphne's shirt, tracing a lazy path over her flat stomach with her fingers. Daphne pressed her lips to Britton's kissing her softly.

As Britton's hand moved lower, Daphne pulled away and stood up, holding her hands out to her wife. When Britton obliged, Daphne tugged her into the house. They made it as far as the couch in the den before giving into the desire burning inside both of them. Some clothes were tossed and others were pushed aside as they moved together, touching each other, frantically searching for release like long lost lovers who'd been reunited.

~

A week later, Britton awoke when the alarm sounded. The space next to her was cool, indicating Daphne had been up for a while. She didn't hear the shower running and wondered if she'd left early for the office. Yawning, she stood up and stretched her muscles, before walking into the bathroom.

Daphne was sitting on the edge of the garden tub with tears on her cheeks. Britton quickly rushed to her side, wrapping her arms around her.

"What's wrong?"

Daphne wiped her face and cradled her head on Britton's shoulder. "I got my period," she whispered.

"Aw, sweetheart. I'm sorry." Britton felt deflated as she held her crying wife. "I love you," she murmured, kissing the top of Daphne's blond head.

"I love you, too," Daphne sighed, lifting her head up. She blew out a frustrating breath and wiped her face once more. "I know Dr. Rooney said it may take a couple of tries, but I guess I believed it would work for us the first time."

"I know, me too." Britton ran her hand up and down Daphne's back.

"I guess I'll go call her office and let them know so we can schedule another round."

"Are you sure you're okay?"

"Yes." Daphne smiled softly, meeting her eyes. "I'll be fine."

Britton kissed her tenderly and pulled away to start the shower. She watched Daphne splash some water on her face and walk out of the room as she stepped under the hot stream. She hated seeing Daphne upset, especially when it was out of her control. The situation made her feel helpless, but deep down she was sad that it hadn't worked. Listening to Daphne talk about their child over the past couple of weeks had raised her hopes a little, too.

Daphne burst through the door, clearing the fog in Britton's head.

"I just spoke to Dr. Rooney," Daphne said loudly. "That woman's a nut," she laughed.

"What did she say?" Britton called over the noise of the shower.

"Not to worry. If every woman got pregnant on the first try, the world would be so overpopulated we'd be walking on top of each other."

"Seriously?" Britton chuckled.

"Yes. I love how she's so direct," Daphne laughed. "Then she asked how I was. Told me not to get discouraged. Anyway, I told her we want to keep going. She tentatively scheduled our next round."

"Sounds good."

"Are you about finished? I need to get in there. I'm already going to be late as it is."

"Yeah. I'll be out in a minute," Britton replied, rinsing the conditioner from her hair.

Chapter 13

Two weeks later, Britton and Daphne went through the process once again. When they walked out of the doctor's office, a cool breeze blew Britton's hair around her shoulders. Fall had finally arrived and she loved every bit of it; the pumpkin-flavored everything, the colors of the leaves, cooler temperatures.

"We should go to lunch," Daphne said, pulling Britton back to reality.

"Really?"

"Yes. I'm not ready to go back to the office. Unless you have a lot to do?"

"No. I'm free." Britton smiled. "And I'd never pass up a lunch date with my beautiful wife," she added.

With the Hardy building behind her, Britton had turned her attention to a new elementary school playground she'd been asked to design. She hadn't wanted to bid on it at first, but the idea that one day her child could be playing on it made her change her mind. Plus, she was still in limbo with the art museum. The mayor had obviously bitten off more than he could chew by getting the approval from the governor before looking for a location and making sure it fit within the city's budget.

Britton pulled out of the parking lot behind her wife's Mercedes just as her cell phone rang. Figuring it was Heather, she let it go to voicemail. She wasn't ignoring her best friend, but it was getting harder and harder to keep everything from her, especially when she needed someone to lean on besides her wife. Watching the pain in Daphne's eyes when they had a negative result tore Britton apart. She didn't like the helplessness that she felt and it had begun to take a toll on her. She knew if she talked to Heather for longer than five minutes at a time, she might accidentally let it slip.

Hearing the chime of the voicemail, she pushed the Bluetooth button on the steering wheel to listen to it.

Britton, it's your sister. Please call me as soon as you get this. Daphne's not answering her phone either and I need to talk to you. It's important.

Britton furrowed her brow in question and sighed as she pushed the button to return her sisters call. They were in the lunchtime traffic downtown, so she had a few minutes.

"What's going on with you and Daphne?" Bridget asked, answering the phone.

"What do you mean? We're fine."

"She hasn't been herself lately. Are you sure everything is fine?"

"Oh, my God. You sound just like our mother," Britton exclaimed. "Everything is great. We've just been really busy lately."

"Don't get me started on Mom. Did you know she had the family attorney call me last week? He wanted to set up a time to meet and discuss my filing for divorce!"

"I tried to tell you to talk to her. She thinks your marriage is over and you're too embarrassed to tell her."

"I'll never get to have kids because that woman is going to drive me to the nuthouse before it ever happens!"

Britton laughed as she pulled into a parking space. "Listen, I'm about to walk into a restaurant—"

"Wait, tell your wife to call me please."

"Tell her yourself," Britton said, pushing the door open.

"She's with you?" Bridget asked.

"Yes. I do go to lunch with my wife when I get the chance." Britton shook her head. "Bridge thinks we're getting divorced."

"What?" Daphne laughed, holding Britton's door open. "Where did that come from?"

"You've been different lately and I was worried something was wrong," Bridget replied, hearing Daphne's voice.

"Honey, we're fine. We've both been working a lot, which is why we're having lunch together. I'll call you later. Maybe we can do something this weekend."

"All right. Enjoy your lunch. Where are you?"

"The Willow Tree," Britton answered.

"They have the best wraps," Bridget murmured.

"Don't forget to call Mom. Better yet, go see her. You two are usually inseparable, you know that right? This is why she's so concerned. You've pulled away from her."

"I know."

"Well, you need to straighten it out, Bridge, or the next thing you know, your divorce announcement will be in the newspaper!"

"If she does that, I'll commit her myself!"

"Oh, my God. She's just like your mother!" Daphne exclaimed when Britton ended the call.

"Yep," Britton laughed."I love you," she said, sliding out of the car and kissing Daphne's lips softly.

"I love you, too." Daphne smiled. "And I really like that new blouse," she added, eyeing the cobalt blue top under Britton's slate gray pantsuit.

"I'm not sure I like that you like it," Britton said, walking towards the restaurant.

"Why?" Daphne questioned, slightly behind her.

Britton stopped at the door and Daphne walked right into her.

"Are you looking at my ass?" Britton chided.

Daphne's cheeks turned a little pink. "Maybe." She shrugged. "I like your ass, especially in those pants." She grinned. "Now, what about your shirt?"

Britton laughed and held the door for her. "The last time you liked one of my shirts, you confiscated it."

"Oh, that happened one time." Daphne rolled her eyes.

"Table for two?" the hostess asked.

"Yes," they replied simultaneously, laughing together as they followed her.

Chapter 14

Two weeks later, Britton found Daphne bawling in the den. She didn't have to ask, she knew by looking at her the insemination had failed again. Britton walked over and sat down, wrapping her arms around Daphne, holding her tightly.

"I don't understand," Daphne sobbed.

"Me either," Britton sighed, kissing the top of her head as a tear ran down her own cheek. Seeing Daphne so sad tore her apart inside.

"Maybe something's wrong with me."

"You're perfect," Britton reassured. "Maybe the third time's a charm?" She shrugged.

"I don't know," Daphne mumbled, burying her face in Britton's neck.

"Do you want to stop?"

"No…I don't know. It's not working."

"Well, if you want to keep going, let's talk to Dr. Rooney and see what she says. She did say it would probably take a few tries." Britton kissed the top of her head again and put her feet up on the ottoman, thankful it was the weekend and neither of them had to go to work. "I'm with you, whatever you want to do," she added.

~

A few days later, Britton and Daphne sat in Dr. Rooney's office, staring around the room as they waited for her to come in.

"Do you think she has a dog or a cat?" Daphne whispered.

"Huh?" Britton raised an eyebrow.

"Is she a cat or dog person?"

Britton shrugged. "Maybe she's neither."

"Most people are one or the other."

"We don't have any pets."

"I like dogs, but it doesn't mean I want one."

"Good, me either," Britton replied matter-of-factly.

"Hello ladies," Dr. Rooney said, entering the room and ending their awkward conversation. She shook hands with both of them before sitting in her desk chair. "You've only had two inseminations and for some people it takes a half dozen or more."

"I don't think we can go through six or more months of this," Britton replied.

"That's why I asked you to come in. Have you given any thought to In Vetro Fertilization? IVF is much more costly, but it can be the better option for someone having trouble with the artificial insemination process. Not that you're having trouble."

"How does that work?" Daphne asked.

"We extract a few eggs from you and fertilize them in the lab. Then a few days later, we insert the fertile embryos into the lining of your uterus. The odds with IVF are about fifty percent, and it can be somewhat painful and uncomfortable. It's definitely not for everyone and often used as a last resort."

Daphne looked at Britton, who squeezed her hand.

"Can we have a few days to decide?" Daphne asked.

"Sure. Take all the time you need."

"When we will need to know for sure?" Daphne asked.

"If you want to start with this current cycle, we'd need to get you on the stimulation medication right away. You'll need to come in for an ultrasound and bloodwork every three days to make sure we stay on track."

"Wow," Britton said.

Dr. Rooney handed them a piece of paper with a calendar printed on it. "This is your twenty-eight day cycle. We're currently right here, which is almost too late to start for this cycle, but you're young, so if we start the stimulation medication today, we will probably have enough stimulation to get a good number of healthy follicles."

"What if that doesn't work?" Britton asked.

"We keep going through the month and try the retrieval next month."

Britton looked at Daphne. "Is this something you want to go through?"

Daphne read the chart again. She'd need to inject herself with two different medications daily, plus get ultrasounds and bloodwork every three days. She took a deep breath and met Britton's eyes. "What do you think?"

"I'll give you two a few minutes," Dr. Rooney interjected before leaving the room.

"Daph, it's your decision, but I will stand by whatever you want to do," Britton said, squeezing her hand. "This seems like a pretty serious process with multiple procedures. Do you want to take some time to think about it?"

"I really want this," Daphne replied as a tear rolled down her cheek.

"Then, let's do it," Britton said, wrapping her arms around her wife, holding her close.

"Can we start today?" Daphne asked when the doctor returned.

"Hell yeah. We need to get an ultrasound done and bloodwork so we can see where you are with your cycle right now. Hopefully, we've caught it early enough to be able to move forward. Otherwise, we'll need to wait."

"Okay." Daphne smiled.

"I'll have one of my nurses get you set up in an exam room and we'll get this party going." Dr. Rooney left the room quickly.

"In all of my life, I've never had a doctor talk to me the way she does," Britton said.

"Me either. I love her. She's down to earth and straight to the point. I'd rather be going through this with her than some clinical robot."

"I agree. Hell yeah!" Britton exclaimed, causing Daphne to laugh hysterically.

~

Britton wrapped her arm around Daphne as they walked out of the doctor's office. "How are you feeling?" she asked.

"A little sore. It hurts when they shove that damn ultrasound wand all around inside of you. I feel like I've already been poked and prodded and we haven't even started the injections."

"I know it won't be easy, but I'll do whatever you need me to do," Britton said. *I hate watching you go through this,* she thought as she pulled Daphne into her arms and held her tightly.

"I think I'm going to call in sick for the rest of the day and head home," Daphne said as she pulled away to get into her car.

"Do you want me to come with you?" Britton asked.

"No. I'll be fine. I'm glad we were able to schedule our appointments at seven in the morning. Hopefully, neither of us will have to take any more time off."

"I'm concerned about you and want to be there for you. This isn't going to be an easy process."

"I know. It's a lot to take in, besides being physically sore. I promise I'll be fine." Daphne put her hand on Britton's cheek before moving in for a kiss.

Britton wrapped her arms around Daphne's waist. "I love you," she whispered against her lips.

"I love you, too." Daphne smiled.

Britton got into her car and turned the key. She didn't want to go back to work. Her mind was racing in a hundred directions. What she really wanted to do was call her best friend and vent over a bottle of wine like they usually did. In all honestly, she was glad no one else knew what they were doing because she didn't think she could go through the highs and lows with her friends and family. Going through them with Daphne was already the hardest thing she'd ever had to do in her life.

Chapter 15

Over the next six days, Britton watched Daphne go through hell. She was unable to give herself the medicated injections, so Britton had had to do it for her. She'd looked away from the tears in Daphne's eyes every morning as she stuck her with both needles. It was the only way she could get through the process without breaking down in front of her.

"God damn it!" Britton yelled towards the sky outside after giving Daphne a painful round of injections and taking her for yet another uncomfortable ultrasound and series of bloodwork. Feeling completely helpless was not something was used to. She picked up a nearby rock, and hurled it out into the bay behind her house. "I hate this entire process," she growled, tossing another small rock as she flopped down onto the bench Daphne loved sitting on.

Thankfully, Daphne was sound asleep upstairs, completely unaware of the breakdown her wife was having. On the eighth day of the calendar, Dr. Rooney gave Daphne an injection of medication to complete the maturation process of the follicles. Then, she scheduled the egg retrieval for forty-eight hours later.

~

The morning of the retrieval, Britton said a silent prayer, hoping this procedure worked as she got out her car and waited for Daphne to get out of the passenger side.

"I'm starting to feel like a cow getting poked and prodded, and injected with hormones," Daphne murmured.

Britton wrapped her arms around her, smelling the scent of their shampoo mixed with her light floral perfume. "You're the most beautiful cow I've ever seen."

Daphne leaned back, smiling at her.

"Hopefully this will all be over soon," Britton murmured.

"I'd be lying if I said I wasn't scared. I haven't been under anesthesia since I was a kid and had my tonsils taken out."

"I'm not leaving your side. I'll be with you through the entire procedure."

Daphne kissed her softly, then pulled away as she grabbed Britton's hand and headed into the building.

~

Britton sat on a stool next to the bed Daphne was lying in, dressed in light blue paper scrubs. The monitor nearby beeped every few seconds as it recorded Daphne's vital signs while she was under the anesthesia.

Dr. Rooney watched the computer monitor as she carefully thread the needle over the top of Daphne's vagina and into the ovary, where she slowly retrieved the follicles, one at a time. As soon as she was finished, one of the nurses immediately took the samples to the lab.

"Everything looks really good," Dr. Rooney said, stepping away to toss her gloves in the trash. "I was able to get six follicles, so we will probably get two to three good eggs from those and hopefully when we add in the sperm later today, we get at least one perfect embryo to implant."

"Okay," Britton croaked before clearing her throat.

"We're going to wake her up in a minute. She's going to need to stay here for an hour so we can keep an eye on her. After that, it's bed rest for the day. She's going to feel mild to severe cramping. I'll write her a prescription to help keep that under control. The best thing she can do is sleep. She'll be back to normal in the morning." Dr. Rooney shook Britton's hand. "We're almost there. Think of this as the seventh inning stretch."

"That's good to know," Britton said.

"I'll see you back here in about seventy-two hours. She'll get her first injection of Progesterone before you leave today. Then, she'll need to give herself one each day for the next five days. And don't forget, no sex."

"Okay," Britton said watching Daphne begin to move around, slowly waking up.

"Daphne? It's Dr. Rooney. We're all finished. Can you hear me?" Dr. Rooney rubbed her shoulder.

Daphne's green eyes flickered a few times before fully opening. Britton stood so she'd be the first thing she saw when her eyes focused. Daphne squeezed her hand lightly and Britton smiled.

"There you are," Dr. Rooney said. "Everything went great. We're all set to move forward in a few days. You're probably going to feel cramping. That's normal.

If it's too much, take the drugs I prescribed. Don't try to tough it out. You'll feel much better tomorrow."

Daphne nodded.

"All right. I'll see you girls soon."

"I love you," Britton whispered, bending to kiss her as soon as the doctor left the room.

"Love you," Daphne murmured.

"Do you feel anything? Does it hurt?" Britton asked, helping her sit up so she could sip some water.

"I feel numb and a little nauseated."

"That's the anesthesia. It'll wear off soon." Britton pushed Daphne's hair gently off her forehead with her finger and kissed her cheek.

~

A few hours later, Daphne experienced some of the worst pain she'd ever felt. Not having difficult menstrual cycles, she'd never dealt with the severe cramping that most women get. She was curled in a ball in the middle of their bed, crying her eyes out. Britton had given her the prescription pain pills, but they were doing nothing to ease the throbbing. She'd finally called Dr. Rooney, who instructed her to put a heating pad over Daphne's lower abdomen, alternating it from there to her lower back.

Britton wrapped Daphne in her arms and held her close with the heating pad half circling Daphne's waist on one side from her belly button to the middle of her lower back. She ran her hand in lazy circles over Daphne's back until she finally cried herself to sleep. Britton held her a little longer, not ready to let go as tears fell down her own cheeks.

"You're my whole world. I hate seeing what this is doing to you. I wish I could take it all away," she whispered.

~

The next day, Daphne felt much better and both women went to work like nothing had changed. Britton had already begun working on the model for the school playground, so that had given her enough work to fill the day.

When she walked into the house that evening, the smell of Mexican food wafted through the air, causing Britton's stomach to rumble loudly.

"Do you ever feed that thing?" Daphne asked, sliding up behind her, wrapping her arms around Britton's waist.

"You're chipper. Are you feeling better?" Britton asked, laying her head back on Daphne's shoulder.

"Yes. Pretty much back to normal after going to the edge of Hell and back."

"You're the strongest person, man or woman, I've ever met. You amaze me," Britton said, turning her head to kiss her.

"It's because I have you in my life. You make me feel like I can be anything...do anything. Maybe it's because you go through life with your hair on fire. I think a little bit of that must have rubbed off on me."

"Something has definitely rubbed off on you," Britton teased playfully.

Daphne pulled away, smacking Britton's tight butt. "Go change. Dinner will be ready soon."

"Who are you? And what have you done with my sweet, innocent wife?" Britton laughed.

"You're a bad influence…see what you've done to me!"

Britton chuckled as she left the room. It felt so good to see Daphne somewhat back to normal with the light back in her eyes. She hoped they really were near the end of this process.

Chapter 16

Britton lay on her back, watching the sun rise. She tried to conjure a blank space in her mind, a place where she was free and clear of all her thoughts. No matter how hard she concentrated, she couldn't get there. Her inner ramblings kept taking her back to Daphne's sad eyes.

Feeling the woman curled up next to her begin to stir, Britton rolled her head to the side, seeing the green eyes looking back at her. "Good morning," Britton said.

"How long have you been awake?" Daphne yawned, having not gotten much sleep either.

"Oh, I don't know. A half hour maybe."

"I tossed and turned all night."

"I know." Britton smiled.

"Sorry."

"It's okay. I'm nervous too, but hopefully this is the end and the beginning, all rolled into one," Britton kissed her softly.

"Do you think we made the right decision going with two? Twins could be a nightmare."

Britton smiled. They'd gone back and forth over how many fertile eggs to transfer and had finally decided on two since they would more than likely never do this again. "We'll be fine," she said.

"What if it doesn't work?" Daphne sighed.

Graysen Morgen

"Let's get through today and see what happens before we start talking about anything else. I love you. We'll figure things out one step at a time. Remember, we're in this together."

"I love you so damn much," Daphne murmured, kissing her.

~

Britton waited patiently next to the exam table where Daphne lay spread-eagle in stirrups with a paper gown and paper sheet covering her. She'd always hated going to the gynecologist and going through all of these procedures with Daphne made her never want to step foot in one again.

"What are you thinking?" Daphne asked, noticing the far off look on her wife's face.

"I'm never going to the lady doctor again."

Daphne laughed. "Seriously? That's what's on your mind?"

"Yes. What did you think I was thinking about?"

"Sex."

Britton guffawed. "Why? I'm not a man. I can go days without thinking about sex."

"Uh huh. Well, if this works, you're going days without sex, period."

"Haven't I already? Why are we all of a sudden talking about sex? I bet that's what you were thinking about."

"No it wasn't," Daphne huffed as her cheeks began to color.

"Sure," Britton teased.

"Well, you lay here with your legs in the air and a breeze blowing over your sacred parts and tell me what your mind conjures up."

"Maybe I should check things out," Britton said, moving to look under the paper sheet.

"Don't you dare!" Daphne said sternly, grasping her arm.

Both women were laughing when Dr. Rooney walked in.

"Should I come back?" the doctor asked with a playful grin.

"No. We're good," Daphne said.

"A little foreplay never hurt anyone," Dr. Rooney said, wiggling her eyebrows.

"Right." Britton nodded.

"Are we ready to get this show on the road?"

"Absolutely," Daphne replied.

"Today is the most difficult process, but it's also much easier on you. Think of it like a pap smear. That's sort of what it will feel like. There's no pain involved, just some mild discomfort for a split second."

"Sounds good. You had me at no pain," Daphne said.

Dr. Rooney's nurse came in with the syringe containing the embryos as she began running the ultrasound camera over Daphne's stomach. She found the image she was looking for
 and placed the nurses hand on the camera so that it didn't move. Then, she inserted the catheter of the syringe through Daphne's opening, past her cervix, and into the middle of the uterine cavity.

Daphne tried to remain as still as possible when she felt the uncomfortable sensation of the catheter moving deeper.

"Hold that image," Dr. Rooney said as she pulled the catheter back and released the embryos. "There they go!"

"That's it?" Britton asked, looking at the screen.

"Yes," Dr. Rooney replied as she slowly removed the catheter.

The nurse immediately took it back to the lab to make sure the embryos had successfully been released. She returned a few second later with a smile on her face.

"Looks like they're both in there." She took one last look at the ultrasound screen, making a few notes and measurements in the computer. "Lie still for about an hour, then you can go. Remember, bed rest for the rest of the day. You can return to light activity tomorrow: walking, sitting at a desk, things like that. No gym, heavy activity, or sex until the pregnancy test. We already have that scheduled for eleven days from now. We do a blood test, which is the most accurate. All of the medications you've been injecting can cause false positives and negatives on urine tests, so avoid the pee sticks."

"Sounds good," Daphne said.

"All right, well, you have about another fifty minutes, so sit back and relax. I'll see you ladies soon."

"How are you feeling?" Britton asked when the door closed behind the doctor.

"Good. That wasn't the most pleasant experience, but it was day and night compared to the last procedure."

"I hate that is has to be like this."

"What do you mean?" Daphne asked.

"So clinical, you know? I wish we could do it at home, in our own bed, like regular people."

Daphne pulled Britton down and kissed her lips. "I wish you and I could make a baby that way too, with you impregnating me in the heat of passion."

"We'd probably have a house full of kids," Britton laughed. "What are we doing for the rest of the day? Did you put your favorite movies on Netflix?" she said, changing the subject.

"You're going to work."

"No, I'm not. We're in this together. You're on bed rest, so that means you only get up to go pee. You can't go up and down the stairs to get food and drinks."

"I was planning on staying in the den."

Britton scrunched her face. "You can lie in our bed and watch TV."

"Are we having a slumber party?" Daphne asked.

"No sex, remember?"

Daphne laughed. "I don't know about you, but my slumber parties never involved sex."

Britton shrugged.

"Were you seriously having sex in high school?"

"No. I was close a couple of times, but my slumber partying took place in college." Britton shook her head. "Frat girls are insane."

"Oh, my God," Daphne giggled. "I definitely don't need to hear anymore."

"If you would've just been honest with me in high school…"

"Yeah, yeah, yeah." Daphne rolled her eyes and smiled.

Chapter 17

"How are you feeling?" Britton questioned, wrapping her arms around Daphne and pulling her close. It had been four days since the implantation and life as they knew it had somewhat gone back to normal. Daphne was still doing the Progesterone injection every night, but other than that, they were back to the waiting game.

"I'd be lying if I didn't say I was a little nervous," Daphne sighed. "But, I'm fine. Seven more days."

Britton kissed her softly. "Come with me. I want to show you something," she said, pulling Daphne down the hallway towards her home office.

Daphne couldn't believe her eyes when she stepped through the doorway. A 3D model of the elementary school playground was sitting on the large table in the middle of the room. The center piece was actually a two-part, broken pirate ship, meant to look like it had been sunk.

"Oh my God, this is amazing, Britton!" Daphne exclaimed.

"The two ship pieces connect at the top by this bridge. There is a ship's wheel, stairs to go to different levels, and multiple porthole openings in each piece. Plus, this gang plank here is actually a slide," Britton said, showing her the pieces. "These here are two separate slides, and there is a flag pole to slide down. The anchor chain is meant to climb down or up. This section here has small hand and foot holds for a simulation rock climbing wall on the outside of the hull. The surrounding pieces of equipment are designed to look like they would be found under the water as well. I made a seahorse teeter totter and a swing set with a shark, fish, and dolphin as the seats. Plus, this here is a large coral reef with the middle open for kids to crawl through and the outside had hand and foot holds to climb up to the top."

"This is unbelievable!"

Britton smiled. "I'm glad you like it. I'm presenting it in the morning. Hopefully, the school board signs off on it without any changes."

"Who's going to construct it?"

"Templeton Fabrication. I actually got involved with them because of the art museum. They build a lot of modern, contemporary designs that most other companies won't touch."

"Maybe our kid will get to play on it one day," Daphne said, smiling brightly.

"Yeah, or I could design a compact version to put here in our backyard." Britton shrugged. "If it's a girl though, she'll probably want a princess castle, which would be pretty cool, too."

"You'd do that?" Daphne questioned.

"What?"

"Design a playground for our house."

"Why not? When the kid outgrows it, I'm sure we'll have grandkids one day who will love it. If it's built right, it will last forever. It may need to be repainted a few times, but it will be there until we decide to remove it."

"I love you," Daphne murmured, wrapping her arms around Britton's neck.

Britton closed her eyes, allowing herself to get lost in the warm and tender feeling of Daphne in her arms with their bodies pressed together.

~

The day after Daphne had her bloodwork done for the pregnancy test, Dr. Rooney's office called, asking her and Britton to come in. Both women made arrangements to go into work late and headed to the doctor's office.

"Do you think it worked?" Daphne asked, feeling a little giddy and really nervous. "I don't think they'd call us in for a negative result, right?"

"I don't know, babe. We'll see in a minute," Britton said, pulling into the parking lot. She was nervous herself and hoped that they were going in to receive good news.

Daphne squeezed Britton's hand gently before walking inside. A few people were in the waiting area, but they were shown to Dr. Rooney's office right away.

"I have a bad feeling," Daphne whispered.

Britton held her hand. "No matter what, we'll get through it."

Daphne nodded just as Dr. Rooney walked into the room.

"Good morning, ladies," she said, sounding less cheery than normal. "I got your results this morning. The implantation didn't take," she sighed, shaking her head.

Large tears dropped from Daphne's eyes, sliding down her cheeks.

"I'm so sorry."

"Where do we go from here? Do you know why it didn't work?" Britton asked.

"I went back over your chart. The lining of a uterus is fairly thin until a woman's cycle begins. Then, the lining begins to thicken and fill with extra blood and so on. This is where a fertile egg embeds itself and grows into a fetus. Some women have low Progesterone levels which cause the lining to be much thinner, therefore the egg is unable to embed itself properly. I believe this is what is happening to you. I noted the lining of the uterus was thinner than normal on several of your ultrasounds, which is why we changed your Progesterone level to help increase it, but it didn't work."

Daphne nodded, still quietly sobbing. Britton moved closer, wrapping her arm around her wife. "Where does this leave us?" she questioned.

"Well…" Dr. Rooney closed the chart. "We can continue the Progesterone injections with the hope that your uterus will eventually thicken enough to sustain a pregnancy during one of your cycles, but the odds are fairly low, definitely less than twenty percent. It could take months, maybe even a year of daily injections."

"I can't," Daphne whispered.

"I'm so sorry," Dr. Rooney said.

"Thank you for everything you've done for us," Britton replied, shaking her hand.

"I'll give you a few minutes." Dr. Rooney walked around her desk, patting Daphne on the shoulder softly before walking out of the room.

"I love you, Daphne. We'll get through this." Britton held her close, kissing the side of her head.

Daphne was devastated. The last thing she'd expected to be told was she couldn't have kids. The world was crashing down around her, crumbling with every tear drop. She tried to calm herself and allowing Britton to cradle her seemed to help. She eventually stopped crying long enough for Britton to get her out of the doctor's office and into the car.

Seeing Daphne so upset broke Britton's heart. She'd been through so much pain and suffering over the last few months only to be told it was almost impossible...Britton couldn't imagine what that was like for Daphne. She was on the outside looking in. Having a child wasn't something she'd thought of since she was a kid like most girls, but the idea of having a family of her own with Daphne was exciting and adventurous, and she'd completely opened her heart to the idea. She wondered where this would leave them. Listening to Daphne sob as she drove them home made her wonder if the woman next to her would ever be the same.

Chapter 18

Britton watched Daphne move like she was on autopilot over the next few weeks, following the same routine of going to work, coming home, eating dinner, and going to bed, every single day. She'd finally stopped crying herself to sleep at night, but her eyes were still full of sorrow. Britton had no idea how to comfort her and take the pain away. Instead of grieving over the loss of a child, Daphne was grieving over the loss of her ability to bear a child. Britton wondered if that loss was somehow more powerful. Knowing you would never get to watch your child grow up had to be one of the hardest things to go through, especially when it wasn't your choice not to have kids.

Britton wanted to call Heather and Bridget, knowing their friends could be a huge help to them right now, but they'd wanted to do this together without everyone's input and sympathy.

Unable to take seeing her wife like this any longer, Britton began researching everything from Daphne's condition to adoption, but she was turned off by the idea that the adoption process could take years and they'd more than likely wind up with an older child. Gay marriage was legal, but adoption for gay couples was still slow going in most states.

Thinking she'd run out of options, Britton ran across a blog one night by two woman who had a similar experience with not being able to get pregnant. Over the course of six months, they blogged daily about their struggle and what they did to overcome it. There were so many blog posts, Britton would need days to get through them, but after the first three entries, she was hooked and stayed up the entire night reading them. The second to last entry was dated eleven months after the blog was started and had a picture of a baby. Then, the final entry was nearly two years later with the picture of another baby next to the child from the previous blog, now a toddler.

Tears rolled down Britton's cheeks as reality sunk in. She knew what to do for her wife, the person she loved more than anything in this world as she pictured Daphne in place of the woman on the screen, holding the small child and smiling back at her.

~

After a long week of barely sleeping and meeting with the builders for the playground, Britton was tired, but she had a newfound sense of euphoria as she waited for Daphne to arrive home. It was Friday and they had the entire weekend to themselves, mostly because Daphne hadn't wanted to do anything in the past month.

Britton was sitting outside on the cushioned bench in front of the bay, the place where she usually found Daphne. A chilly breeze blew through the air, pushing her hair around her shoulders. Most of the ducks had already headed south for the upcoming winter, but a few still hung around, looking up at her to toss them some treats.

"Sorry, guys. Daphne usually feeds you, not me," she uttered, staring out at the small wakes trailing behind each of them. She turned around, facing the house when she heard the door open. "Hey, you," she said, smiling at her wife.

"I picked up takeout. I hope you don't mind," Daphne said, walking out to her. "I didn't feel like cooking."

"Come here." Britton nodded, pulling Daphne down into her lap. "Your ducks are hungry," she said, kissing her softly.

"I have no idea why they didn't leave with the others. They won't survive the winter if they stay here," Daphne replied, brushing Britton's hair back over her shoulder.

"How was your day?"

"Boring. We have inventory soon, so I pretty much stared at printouts of negative-on-hand products all day. What about you?"

"The builder ran into a snag with the playground, so I had to go straighten that out, but I came home a couple of hours early."

"You did? What for?"

"I was up all night."

"Are you feeling okay?" Daphne asked, kissing her forehead.

"I'm fine." Britton cleared her throat nervously.

"Are you sure? You're acting funny."

"I haven't slept much in the last couple of days." Britton fidgeted with the hem of Daphne's shirt.

"Honey, what's wrong?" Daphne asked, lifting Britton's chin up so that she could look into her eyes.

Britton swallowed the lump in her throat. "I've been doing a lot of thinking and soul searching. I know what you went through was the hardest thing you've ever faced in your life, but—"

"I've thought about adoption too. It can take years and then maybe never happen for couples like us," Daphne sighed.

Britton shook her head. "That's not what I meant."

"Okay…" Daphne ran her hand through Britton's hair.

"I want to have our child," Britton blurted out.

"What?"

"I'm serious. I've thought about it a lot, and I want to do this…for us."

"Really?"

"Yes." Britton smiled. "I want a family with you."

"Oh, my God," Daphne cried. "I love you so much."

"I love you, too."

"Are you sure you want to go through all of that? What if you have the same problems I had? This is a lot to take in."

"Actually, that's why I haven't slept in two nights. I ran across a blog about these two women and how they successfully did artificial insemination at home with no doctors. Then, I researched everything I could find about the process."

"Wow."

"If I do this, I don't want it to be a medical procedure in a stale, loveless environment. These women did it at home with no problem."

"What if you're like me?" Daphne murmured.

"Most couples that did this got pregnant within two to six months, so if nothing happens, then we'll move on to adoption or surrogacy."

"You really have done your homework," Daphne said with surprise.

"I'll show you everything this weekend and if we want, we can get started on Monday. According to my cycle, my ovulation time should be in about a week. We'll need to go buy those pee stick things so we know which day to actually do it."

"What about the donor?" Daphne asked.

"Hopefully, he is still available, if not, we'll go with choice number two."

Daphne's head was spinning. This was the last thing she'd ever expected Britton to say to her. "I can't wrap my head around all of this. Are you sure you want to do this?" she whispered.

"Yes. I wouldn't have brought it up if I wasn't." Britton kissed her. "I love you," she murmured against her lips.

"Britton, you are everything to me. Absolutely everything," she said, holding her tightly.

Chapter 19

The following week, Daphne and Bridget ordered the frozen sperm to be sent to their house, purchased a box of ovulation test sticks, and found a package of small syringes for baby medication, which would work for the insertion.

"We're all set," Britton said when the cryogenic container arrived a few days later.

"Don't you think we should practice?" Daphne asked nervously.

"How hard is it to suck the stuff up into the syringe and squirt it inside?" Britton said. "Oh, that doesn't sound appealing at all," she grimaced.

Daphne laughed. "We only get one shot at this, so we sort of need to know what we're doing."

Britton rolled her eyes.

"Did you pee on the stick?"

"Mostly on my hand, but the stick had a smiley face," Britton answered.

"Gross."

"They don't exactly come with instructions on which way the stream will go!" Britton exclaimed. "Come on, let's get this going."

Daphne followed her to their bedroom upstairs. She watched as Britton undressed and got up on the bed.

"Make sure you use the gloves or your fingers will be frost bitten," Britton said.

"How the hell am I supposed to do this with these giant fucking gloves?" Daphne muttered, trying to open the container with the set of extra large welding gloves Britton had purchased. "Damn it," she hissed as her hand slipped.

"Here we go," Britton whispered when she finally got the lid off and pulled out a tiny little vial.

"Oh, this stinks!" Daphne wrinkled her nose as she opened the vial.

"You're not supposed to inhale it!"

Daphne's eyes shot her daggers as she slowly pulled the plunger back on the syringe, sucking the milky liquid up until it was full. Then, she stepped closer to the bed where Britton was lying spread-eagle.

"Make sure you get the right hole."

Daphne raised an eyebrow. "Do you want to do this yourself?"

"Hell no. I'm not touching that stuff."

"Then lie there and shut up," Daphne growled.

Britton held her breath, barely feeling the tiny syringe enter her. Daphne inserted as far as she could and tried to push the plunger forward, but it was stuck. She balanced on her knees between Britton's legs in the middle of the bed, holding the syringe with one hand, as she forcefully pushed the plunger to get it unstuck.

"Shit," she exclaimed as the plunger raced forward, squirting the freshly thawed sperm inside of Britton at breakneck speed. Daphne panicked, pulling the syringe out quickly, spraying the remainder of the liquid onto their comforter. "Oh, fuck!"

"What's wrong? Did you lose the syringe? Is it inside of me? Get it out!" Britton exclaimed, freaking out.

Daphne laughed hysterically, holding up the syringe. "The damn end of this thing got stuck. I shot the sperm in there at about a hundred miles an hour!"

Britton chuckled. "Aren't you supposed to do it very slow and gently?"

"Yep." Daphne shook her head. "Don't move."

"Why? It probably won't work. I'm sure they're all dead."

"I got it on the bed," Daphne said, moving to grab a towel.

"Oh, gross!" Britton rolled to the side to be away from the wet spot in the middle of their comforter. "Don't use a towel. Put this thing in the washing machine, pronto!"

Daphne tried not to laugh, but the entire experience was hilarious. "This was definitely not a clinical process," she giggled.

"Yeah, no kidding." Britton smiled, shaking her head as she help Daphne roll their comforter up.

"I will be surprised if that worked," Daphne said, shaking her head as she carried the blanket out of the room.

"Me too!" Britton called back. "There's always next month."

~

Britton didn't need to worry about taking a pregnancy test, her period was on time two weeks later.

She and Daphne laughed it off and by the time her cycle rolled around again, they were ready.

"We need to hurry," Daphne said. "Your sister was expecting us ten minutes ago!"

"Bridget and her party can wait. We're making a baby here!" Britton chided as she got on the bed.

"Maybe you should take your costume off first," Daphne laughed, looking down at Britton dressed in her gangster costume.

"Damn it!" Britton got off the bed and removed her clothing. "I needed to make sure it fit. Leave it to Bridget to make her Halloween party themed this year!"

"I like the gangster and flapper idea. Besides, I think you look hot in your suspenders and fedora."

"Yeah, well I won't be so hot once you fill me up with seminal fluid."

"When you put it that way..." Daphne shivered and scrunched her face.

"Can we get this going or what?"

"All right, all right." Daphne opened the container and filled the syringe with the liquid from the vial. "I can't believe how rancid this smells."

"I'll take your word for it."

Daphne smiled, then scooted forward, inserting the syringe and the pushing the plunger forward. She waited a minute, and pulled it back out. "All done. Are you supposed to lie there or anything? Bridget's cell phone rang on the dresser nearby. "That's probably your sister."

"Tell her we're in the throes of passion and will be there when we get there," Britton chided. "Wait, better yet, hand me the phone."

"No. Go get dressed," Daphne said.

"I thought I had to wait."

Daphne shrugged. "Dr. Rooney made me wait ten minutes, I think."

Britton sat up. "It's probably fine. It's been at least five."

Daphne sent Bridget a quick text saying they were on their way. "You lie there a little longer. I'll go ahead and get dressed."

As soon as ten minutes had passed, Britton got up and quickly put her costume back on."I like you like this," she said, sliding up next to her wife. Daphne was dressed like a 1920's flapper with a low-cut, short dress, high heels and long dangling earrings. Her hair was rolled into buns on both sides of her head and tucked under a hat. She finished the look with a fake cigarette stick.

"Really?" Daphne laughed, pulling on her suspenders.

"The costumes this year will definitely come in handy," Britton grinned, leaning forward and kissing her passionately.

"We're going to be late," Daphne said, playfully pulling away from her.

"We're already late." Britton wiggled her eyebrows.

"Did you forget what we just did?"

"Eww...thanks for the mood killer." Britton scrunched her face.

~

When they arrived at the party, Bridget made a beeline for both of them, yanking them down the hallway before anyone noticed they were there.

"What the hell?" Britton grumbled.

"I talked to Mom," Bridget said, raising her eyebrows.

"How did that go?" Daphne asked.

"I told her Wade and I aren't getting divorced. Of course, she rambled on and on. I don't think she believes me!"

Britton laughed.

"Damn it, Britton! It's not funny."

"Did you tell her you guys weren't ready for kids, but you want them down the road?" Daphne asked.

"No, she wouldn't let me get a word in. She and Daddy are outside mingling. Don't mention anything about this."

Britton rolled her eyes.

"Come on, there's wine in the kitchen," Bridget said.

"You can't have alcohol, remember?" Daphne whispered as they walked behind Bridget.

"This party just got even better," Britton huffed under her breath, refusing when her sister tried to pour her a glass of merlot.

"You don't want anything?" Bridget asked.

"No. She wasn't feeling well earlier," Daphne interjected.

"What's going on with the two of you? I barely see you anymore," she said to Daphne. "And Heather told me she hasn't seen you in weeks." She looked at Britton. "Is everything okay?"

"Yes. We're fine. We've been working a lot and you know when we're alone we barely come up for air." Britton grinned.

"I've never been happier in my life. Things are great," Daphne added.

"So, what about you guys? Are you thinking of having kids anytime soon?"

"Have we met?" Britton guffawed.

Bridget laughed. "Yes. I know you and your views on the world." She eyed Britton and turned to Daphne. "I'm still surprised that you are married to her, but it's obvious in the way you look at each other and the way Britton boasts about your voluptuous sex life. Besides, I know you want kids. You used to talk about it all the time when we were younger."

"Trust me, with the way this family operates, when and if we decide to have kids will be our decision. You all will find out when he or she is about to enter this world," Britton stated.

"I don't blame you. When mom found out you guys eloped, I thought she was going to lose it. I see why you did it though. She's making me crazy."

"You need to sit her down, away from any distractions, and be honest with her. Tell her that taking over the family business is important to you right now and when you're ready, you'll have children. Don't be scared to put your damn foot down, Bridge, you're an adult and this is your life," Britton said.

Bridget looked at Daphne who shrugged. "She's rubbing off on you," she said to Britton.

Britton opened her mouth to comment and Daphne lurched forward, stomping on her toe.

"Ouch!"

"Sorry, I lost my balance. These cheap ass heels are hurting my feet," Daphne replied.

"Well, take the damn things off!" Britton shook her head, giving her wife an odd look.

"Hey! I wondered if I was going to see you," Heather cheered, giving Britton a hug. "Every time I see you, you're going like your hair's on fire!" she added as they walked outside together.

"I know. That playground has been a handful and the mayor has had me chasing my damn tail for the last six weeks. I think we're finally ready to move forward, though. How are things with you?"

"Good. You were right about that new dentist, by the way. She's a lesbian."

"No way!" Britton chuckled. "I knew it. No one has ever cleaned my teeth that thoroughly before."

"The girls in the office don't know. They still think she's after the old fat toad we work for."

"How did you find out?"

"She knows you're my best friend, so she started asking about you more and more. I guess she didn't see your wedding band, which is pretty hard to miss. Anyway, she finally asked me if you were seeing anyone."

Britton smiled. "What did you say to her?"

"Well, I point blank asked her if she was gay and she said yes, but she's not really out to people. She thinks you're hot, but I told her you were married to my cousin, and I showed her a picture of the two of you. She thinks Daphne's even hotter."

"Don't let Daphne get her teeth cleaned there. I'd have to scratch that chick's eyes out."

Heather laughed hysterically.

"What's so funny over here?" Greg said, sliding up and wrapping his arm around Britton.

"What the hell are you wearing?" Britton asked, eyeing his costume. He was dressed as a giant fedora.

"I'm a hat," he said proudly, pulling away from her to show off his outfit.

"What?"

"We have two parties to go to and we'd already picked our costumes before Bridget sent out the invitations with the theme. So, instead of the Cat and the Hat, we're the flapper cat and the gangster hat," Heather replied.

Britton looked at both of them, noticing for the first time that Heather truly was dressed like a cat in a flapper dress. "You know it's the Cat *in* the Hat, right?"

Heather and Greg looked at each other, then burst with laughter.

"Oops!" Heather shrugged.

"Hey guys, you look cute!" Daphne stepped closer, hugging Heather and Greg.

"They're the flapper cat and the gangster hat," Britton added, moving closer to her, but keeping her feet away from the treacherous heels. "I'm not going to be able to go nine months without alcohol," she whispered into Daphne's ear, before kissing her cheek.

Daphne smiled at her. "I knew our costumes were too plain," she said pursing her lips.

"You guys look great," Heather retorted.

"Hey, Britt, why aren't you a flapper too?" Greg teased.

"I'll wear it if you will," she shot back with a wink.

"That sounds like a bet."

Britton shrugged.

Daphne and Bridget finally decided to head home an hour later. Britton had had enough of mingling.

"I can't do it. There is no way I'm going to make it nine months without drinking," she babbled on the way to the car.

"Will you slow down?" Daphne called from behind her. "These fucking shoes are killing me."

"Why are you still wearing them?"

"I don't know." Daphne stopped in the middle of the driveway and held onto Britton's shoulder as she removed the heels. Her feet felt a hundred times better as they made their way to the car. She spotted the neighbors trashcan by the road and jogged over, tossing the shoes inside.

"Did you really just do that?" Britton laughed.

"Get in the car," Daphne hissed.

Chapter 20

Britton sighed when she awoke in the middle of the night with cramps. She knew from reading that blog it could take several months, but she wasn't sure she and Daphne could handle many more months of let downs.

"Is everything okay?" Daphne asked when Britton crawled back into their bed.

"Yeah," Britton whispered. "Aunt Flow arrived."

Daphne nodded.

"I think we need a change of scenery. We've been at this for months. It would do us some good to clear our heads and relieve some stress," Britton said, wrapping her arms around her wife.

"What do you want to do?"

"Our anniversary is coming up in a couple of weeks. I was thinking of going back to Watch Hill," she replied, thinking about the beautiful beach and seaside cottage where they eloped.

"Really?" Daphne smiled. "I was thinking the same thing, but it's the middle of the week."

"I own my business and you have plenty of vacation time," Britton replied.

"It's a plan then."

~

Britton drove along the scenic route, heading south, while Daphne watched the expanse of trees with occasional glimpses of the coast, go by. The salty air tickled her senses when they finally arrived. She got out of the car, stretching like a Cheshire cat.

"I love it here," Daphne murmured, walking around the car.

"I do too. Maybe we should move," Britton said, grabbing her hand.

"I'm stuck where I am. I don't think your father has plans to expand to the south. Besides, we have a beautiful coastal house already."

"I know. I think the atmosphere here is completely different. That's why we love it so much," Britton added as they walked inside the Victorian Manor.

"Mrs. and Mrs. Prescott!" the man behind the counter exclaimed. "How are you?"

"We're great. How is your father?" Britton asked, speaking about the retired judge who owned the property and officiated their wedding on the beach.

"I'm afraid he isn't well. He had to have a pacemaker and two stints put in."

"Aww. Please tell him we are thinking of him," Daphne replied. "This place is very near and dear to our hearts. We think about it quite often actually."

Britton nodded in agreement.

"Thank you. I'll make sure to tell him. So, we have the Sea Gate Cottage all ready for you. Please enjoy your stay with us," he said, handing her the papers to sign and the keys to their rental cottage.

Britton and Daphne walked back outside with smiles on their faces, and gathered their luggage from the car. The small, beachfront house was just as Daphne remembered. It had been two years since they stood on the nearby beach, freezing in the cold wind as they said their vows in a private ceremony that was everything they'd wanted, away from the large extravaganza of a wedding their families had put together, which had taken place a couple of weeks later.

"I could stay here forever," Daphne mumbled as she set her suitcase down and looked out the large floor to ceiling windows.

"Me, too." Britton wrapped her arms around her from behind. "Are you hungry?"

Daphne moved her butt against Britton's crotch.

"I meant for food," Britton giggled. "I was thinking of going to that little restaurant down the road. The one with the amazing seafood bisque."

"Oh, yeah. I remember that place. Let's walk along the beach."

"Great idea." Britton kissed her cheek.

~

After dinner, Britton and Daphne strolled along on the damp, beach sand, looking out at the crashing waves and sky full of stars.

"I can't believe how cold it got," Daphne shivered.

Britton wrapped her arm around her, holding her close. "We're almost there," she replied, spotting their cottage. "We need to make it a point to visit here in the summer."

"No kidding," Daphne laughed.

Britton pulled her to a stop in the middle of the beach. "Here we are, two years later," she said, holding her arms out. She was standing in the exact spot where they'd said 'I Do'. "I wouldn't change it for the world. I love you more every day."

"Me either. You're my whole world, Britton." She wrapped her arms around her wife's neck, kissing her passionately.

Britton ran her hands under the back of Daphne's thin jacket and blouse, feeling the warmth of her silky smooth skin.

"We should probably go inside before I pull your clothes off right here," Daphne whispered against her lips.

"If it wasn't so cold, I'd be game," Britton teased.

"Somehow, I think you'd do it either way." Daphne grinned, grabbing her hand and pulling her towards the cottage.

"Should I start a fire?" Britton asked as they walked inside.

"No. I think we'll be fine," Daphne replied, removing her shoes and jacket. "I have plenty of plans to keep you warm."

Britton raised an eyebrow as she shed her own jacket and shoes.

Daphne stepped closer, working with Britton to remove the rest of their clothing before pressing their naked bodies together, sharing another long kiss. Britton pulled away, grabbing Daphne's hand, tugging her over to the bed, where they lay down together side by side, trading gentle caresses and languid kisses.

Britton went along as Daphne moved over her, dipping her head to lick and suck each of her breasts as she ran her hands over the smooth skin of Britton's body.

Her hips rose on their own accord, searching for contact as her blood began to race. Daphne sat up.

"Roll over," she whispered, kissing Britton hard.

Obliging, Britton turned to her stomach. Daphne moved back over her, pushing Britton's chestnut locks to the side as she ran her lips over her shoulders and back. When she reached the small of Britton's back, Daphne replaced her lips with her tongue and ran it up the center of her spine in a slow, steady motion.

"Are you trying to kill me?" Britton gasped.

"I want you to feel like you're going to come without me touching you," Daphne murmured, licking the outside edge of her ear.

Britton was on such a euphoric high, she felt like she was going to disintegrate. "I'm close," she mumbled, trying to regain her composure.

Daphne pushed her back over and kissed her once more, exuding as much passion as she could muster in that one kiss. Her thigh slipped between Britton's legs, coming in contact with her wet center. Britton moaned, grinding herself hard against Daphne's leg as she raised her hips. Daphne pulled her leg back, causing Britton to whimper.

"I'll be right back," Daphne whispered.

Britton tried to clear the fog in her head.

Daphne returned a minute later with the specimen vial from the cryogenic container and one of the small syringes they used for insemination.

"Isn't it too early?" Britton questioned, still trying to come back to reality.

Daphne shrugged. "I don't know, but I think this is the best time to try it, when we're not expecting it. I read that stimulation is the best thing you can do to help things along. Why not do it right in the middle of making love?"

Britton nodded, then smiled. "Why not?" she said, spreading her legs.

Daphne pulled the plunger back, sucking up the milky liquid from the vial. Then, she moved between Britton's legs, inserting it slowly. She waited a few minutes, then removed the syringe, tossing it on the floor and she moved over Britton, sliding her hand down her body as she kissed her.

Feeling Daphne's hand between her legs, Britton broke the kiss. "Are you sure you want to do this?"

"I'm not going inside." Daphne smiled. "Relax."

Britton met her lips for another searing kiss as Daphne's fingers circled her clit. It didn't take long for her euphoric state to return. Her hips moved in motion with Daphne's hand, driving her closer and closer to the edge, until her body finally released the pent up climax she'd been holding.

Britton let out a guttural moan before her body went limp under Daphne, who slowly moved away, curling up against her side.

"That was…" Britton tried to speak.

"Incredible? Mind-blowing?" Daphne teased.

"Just the beginning," Britton finished, rolling on top of her.

~

Britton and Daphne spent the next two days in their cottage, hiding from the cold weather and making love to keep warm. Neither woman wanted to leave when Thursday morning arrived.

"Do we have to go?" Daphne pouted, looking out the windows as the sun began to rise over the ocean. "It's so peaceful here."

Britton held her tightly. "I wish we could stay right here, just like this, forever."

"Me too. Maybe we should come here every anniversary." Daphne smiled, rubbing her hand over Britton's cheek.

"Deal." Britton grinned, kissing her palm. "Come on, Mrs. Prescott. We need to get on the road if you're going to make it to work," she added, looking at their suitcases before her eyes landed on the cryogenic container. "I was wondering why you needed to bring your own suitcase."

"I wasn't sure if you want to do it here or not, but I also didn't want it to be planned."

Britton nodded. "Everything happens for a reason. I think this was the perfect time for it."

Daphne smiled. "Are you going to your office when we get home?"

"Yes. I need to at least make an appearance and make sure a chaotic disaster hasn't happened with the playground while I was gone. It's supposed to be completed next week."

"That's good. I can't wait to see it."

"I also need to get started on the models for the art museum. Those are going to take probably three weeks to build."

"Looks like you have a busy month ahead of you," Daphne said, moving on top of Britton and sitting up to straddle her.

"You're playing with fire," Britton whispered.

"Good. I like it hot," Daphne said seductively, bending down to kiss her.

Chapter 21

At the end of the following week, Britton had finally started working on the model for the art museum. She had a half dozen sketches showing the intricate detail of the building itself, scattered all over the large table in her office, as well as detailed drawings of the three floors and the individual exhibit rooms. The diamond-shaped building was designed with the middle open to the ceiling so people could look over the railing on each level at the art pieces on the ground and hanging in the air. It also had a gift shop on the main floor and a tapas restaurant on the top floor.

The scaled model of the building with the parking lot and cut away sections of each level was going to take at least four weeks for her to complete, but with the Christmas and New Year's holidays coming up, she'd have at least five, maybe six weeks before she would need to unveil the model at city hall, giving her plenty of time.

"Can we fast forward to next year already?" Kathleen said, walking into Britton's office.

"I wish," Britton mumbled as she worked. She was writing down all of her material measurements so she could go in the back and cut them out of the project wood she used for her models. "Did the new supplies I ordered come in?"

"Yes. I didn't open the box yet. What is it?"

"Exterior siding to give this model a faux stucco look without me working with clay for three days, and a bunch of interior décor," Britton said as she stood up. "I'll be in the back for the rest of the day, so take all of my calls, please."

"Sure. Would you like me to order in lunch?"

"You read my mind." Britton smiled. "A wrap and smoothie or soup and salad are fine with me," she added, walking out of her office with the sketches and measurements.

~

The back room of Prescott Designs was fairly large with project wood sheets and piles of micro-cut strip pieces in different thicknesses, shapes, and lengths along one side. Various paints, glue, clay, and other building materials were on shelves on the opposite side of the room, and scaled-saws and other equipment were on a large table in the middle. The far back wall had a large cabinet full of interior décor: staircases, tables, chairs, rugs, desks, doors, and other various pieces.

Britton walked into the room, set her papers on the table, and began pulling out sheets of wood to cut. Depending on the model, she used different types of materials from foam-filled board to clay, but most of the time, the framework of her models was made of wood. Although it was more expensive and more difficult to work with, she found wood to be the most sturdy, especially for the frame of a building with multiple floors. The addition of paint and texture also made it look the most professional.

She spent hours measuring the wood and making precise cuts for all of the interior walls, plus the exterior walls, the roof and base for each floor. She'd also trimmed out the doorways on each piece. Then, she cut the columns that would hold up each floor. With the frame completely cut out, she decided to call it a day. Kathleen had already left, closing the office over an hour ago.

Britton zipped her leather jacket and wrapped her scarf around her neck before walking out into the cold air. Christmas was still four weeks away, but the crisp bite in the temperature made her wonder if they were going to get a dusting of snow early this year. She didn't mind the winter, but snow on the roads was a different story. People seemed to drive as if they'd completely forgotten how to do it overnight.

As soon as she started the car, Britton pushed the Bluetooth button and said, "Call Heather." Then, she drove off as she waited for the call to go through.

"Hey, I was just thinking about you," her best friend answered.

"Hmm, maybe I'm psychic or something," Britton replied.

"Tell me what the future holds for me, Madame," Heather laughed.

"A bottle of wine and a husband with a stiff one."

"Damn, I was hoping for a massage and a weekend away," Heather said.

"A psychic isn't a genie, hun."

Heather guffawed. "Isn't that the truth. Speaking of massage, there is a new place downtown that everyone is talking about. I was thinking of trying it out. Do you want to go with me?"

"If they drown you in mud and bitch slap you with palm fronds, hell no."

Heather giggled, remembering the spa day she and Britton had shared before Britton's wedding. "No, I think this place is a little different. They do have seaweed wraps and things like that, but nothing as extravagant as that other place we went to."

"Does the massage come with a happy ending?" Britton teased.

"What's that? I'll call and ask."

Britton nearly drove off the road she was laughing so hard. "No, don't call them! Ask Greg. Doesn't he get massages?"

"Yeah, once or twice a year for his back. He gets the deep tissue kind that hurt like hell," Heather said. "Wait, he just got home. Hold on a second."

Britton downshifted and came to a stop at a red light near her house. When the light changed, she headed further down the road and turned down the street that led to her neighborhood.

"You ass!" Heather exclaimed with laughter as she came back on the phone. "If you want a happy ending, you go right ahead!"

"I'm about to have a happy ending, as soon as I walk inside," Britton replied, seeing Daphne's car in the garage.

"Thanks for telling me," Heather snickered. "Tell my cousin I said hello and get back to me on the massage if you want to go."

"All right." Britton ended the call and headed inside with a huge smile on her face. She found Daphne in the den, finishing putting up the rest of the Christmas decorations. They'd started that weekend with putting the

Christmas tree in the formal living room, completely covered with an array of decorations and wrapping red and green garland around the rail of the staircase. Daphne was adding a reindeer and a snowman on the fireplace mantel to hold their stockings and a few other things here and there.

"You look happy," Daphne said, walking over to her.

"Your cousin says hi."

"I see." Daphne nodded, wrapping her arms around Britton's neck. "Is this beautiful smile for me or my cousin?"

"Heather wants to go get massages at this new place and I asked her if they were offering happy endings. She was going to call and find out," Britton chuckled.

"Oh, God. I don't know how she could be that naive, especially after hanging around you all of these years."

"I know, right." Britton grinned, sliding her arms around Daphne's waist. "I could use a happy ending after the long day that I've had," she said, wiggling her eyebrows before kissing her softly.

"You're on your own with that one. Aunt Flow stopped by for a visit."

"Wonderful," Britton sighed. "How was the rest of your day?"

"Shitty. We are changing over the inventory scanning program and New Bedford is first. I've been asked to go help out, so I'll be out of town next week."

"The entire week?"

"No. I think it's Wednesday to Friday."

"That sucks. Will you be driving back and forth or staying there?"

"No. I'll be in a hotel."

"Hmm, maybe I'll sneak up there one night," Britton said, kissing her.

"That would be nice," Daphne replied, lingering against her lips. "Speaking of massages, I think you should go. It would probably be good for you. I know they relax me physically and mentally."

"Maybe I'll do it Wednesday night after work since you'll be gone."

"Do they do seaweed wraps? Those are divine," Daphne murmured, kissing her again.

"Yes and I'm not letting them turn me into a sushi roll."

Daphne laughed, pulling away. "You're a mess."

Chapter 22

After having spent the previous evening getting molded like a piece of human clay at the spa, Britton was feeling good. She drank a cup of coffee and ate a banana, heading to the office to work on her model. She'd missed having Daphne next to her, which caused her to toss a turn most of the night.

"You have a delivery," Kathleen called out when she heard Britton walk in.

"I bet it's the rest of the interior décor. The last box only had part of it," she said, cutting the tape with a pair of scissors.

The box had tiny, fake pictures in frames, statues, and a few other things which were all molded plastic pieces that were basically décor for a fancy doll house. Britton looked at each one carefully, before putting them all back in the box.

"I'll be in the back if you need me," she said, carrying the small box down the hall. The smell of freshly cut wood and modeling glue permeated the air in the back room. Britton felt her stomach roll as she set the box on the floor next to the other one.

Figuring her breakfast hadn't mixed well, she shrugged it off and walked to the other end of the table where her model pieces were slowly coming together.

She sat on the stool and opened the glue, preparing to put the interior walls in place for the second and third levels.

She'd finished securing the first piece when her stomach turned again. Feeling like she was going to hurl, Britton ran to the bathroom down the hall, just making it as she began puking. She eventually stopped dry-heaving after a minute or two and stood up, washing her face and rinsing her mouth in the sink. As soon as she went back what she was doing, her belly flopped again, causing her to rush back to the bathroom.

Finally getting her stomach somewhat under control, despite feeling severely nauseated, Britton hurried through gluing the rest of the interior pieces for the second floor and began working on the top level.

~

Kathleen walked into the back room a few hours later with the lunch menu from a Chinese place down the street from their office. "I'm going to the Little Dragon for lunch. Do you want anything?"

"No," Britton said, shaking her head. "I've been sick all morning. I went out for Mexican last night after the spa and I think I ate something bad."

"That sucks. I hope you feel better."

"Me too. I'd go home, but I need to get these walls done so I can start painting everything on Friday."

Kathleen nodded. "I'll be back in a bit."

As soon as she was gone, Britton's stomach lurched again. She sat down, feeling light-headed and a little dizzy. "What the hell did I eat?" she mumbled, trying to get her bearings. When the sensation passed, she grabbed her cell phone and scrolled through her contacts. A minute later, Heather answered.

"Hey, are you sick?" Britton asked. "I think I ate something bad last night."

"I was thinking the same thing. I woke up with the shits, but they're gone now...I hope. I haven't tried to eat anything, so we'll see," Heather said.

"I've been puking my guts out," Britton huffed. "I feel like calling that restaurant and cussing them out!"

"Good luck with that. They barely speak English," Heather retorted.

"Great." Britton shook her head. "I haven't had food poisoning in years."

"Me either," Heather replied. "Hey, I have a patient coming back. I'll call you tonight."

Britton ended the call and set her phone to the side before going back to her model.

~

That night, she talked to Daphne, who had nothing but sympathy for her and told her to drink plenty of fluids and eat crackers. She felt too nauseated to eat or drink. Simply thinking about ingesting anything made her want to puke her guts out. She finally fell asleep while watching a Christmas-themed, romantic comedy on the Hallmark channel, and woke up the next morning feeling just the same.

She was barely out of the bed before her stomach churned, causing her to rush to the bathroom. At this point, she'd barely drank anything and hadn't eaten in twenty-four hours, so she was mostly sitting on her knees in front of the toilet, dry-heaving.

Feeling a little better, she got up off the floor and got into the shower. When she finally got out, she was exhausted and still nauseated. She'd hoped the shower would help ease some of her discomfort, but she actually felt worse. She towel-dried her hair and went downstairs to drink some water with lemon, which she read helped calm a stomachache, but as soon as she opened the refrigerator her stomach lurched, causing her to throw up in the sink.

Knowing she didn't have the energy to drive herself to the office, she called Kathleen and let her know she wasn't coming in. Then, she reluctantly called Daphne.

"Good morning. I was just thinking about you," she answered. "How are you feeling?"

"Really bad. I can't even keep water down. I'm too weak to do anything but lay in the bed."

"Oh, my God, Britton. I'm coming home right now."

"You don't need to do that. I'll be fine."

"You'll get dehydrated. Keep trying to drink water," Daphne urged.

"I know. I'm going back to bed. I'm sorry I can't come up there tonight like we'd planned."

"Baby, I'm worried about you. Are you sure you don't want me to come home?"

"No. It'll pass," Britton sighed. "I'm going to go back to bed and try to sleep it off."

"All right. I love you. Call me if anything changes."

Britton ended the call and went back upstairs.

~

Lunchtime came and went without Britton moving a muscle. She'd slept on and off, and had barely drunk a few sips of the water on the nightstand. She felt absolutely miserable as she huddled under the covers. The sound of the alarm beeping, meaning a door had opened in the house, brought her to attention. She nearly fell out of bed. The monitor on the wall blinked for door number three, which was coming from the garage.

"Hello?" she called out.

"It's me," Daphne replied, coming up the stairs.

"What are you doing home?" Britton questioned, feeling somewhat better as her eyes landed on her wife's face.

"You're sick and you need me. They have plenty of people working on that changeover. I need to be here, with you," she replied, sitting on the edge of the bed and hugging Britton. "Baby, you have a fever," she exclaimed, putting her hand on Britton's forehead. "Have you drunk anymore water?"

"Not really."

"I think you should go to the hospital," Daphne said.

"It's food poisoning. There's nothing they can do."

"If you're dehydrated, they can give you fluids. Will you please go, for me? I'm worried about you."

"All right," Britton sighed as she sat up.

Daphne watched her change into a pair jeans and a cable-knit sweater that hugged her small breasts and slender waist. Then, she pulled on a pair of leather boots. "You look like you're going on a date and not to the hospital," she teased.

"I can't go out looking like bum," Britton replied, running her hand through her hair and pushing it over her shoulder. "I'm ready when you are."

"I guess I can go like this," Daphne said, looking down at the office attire she was wearing.

Britton smiled. "You'd look great in a paper sack."

Daphne laughed.

Chapter 23

The hospital wasn't too crowded for a weeknight. Daphne sat in the waiting area while Britton signed in. The local news was playing on the TV nearby and the elderly couple across from her seemed to be more interested in her than anything else in the room.

"It shouldn't be long. There are only two people ahead of me," Britton said, sitting down and squeezing her hand.

"That's good. I hate hospitals," Daphne muttered.

"Did you hear about that?" Britton said, nodding towards the TV, where the news anchors were discussing a story about a dog who ran away and returned home a year later.

"Do you want to get a dog?" Daphne asked.

"No. Why would I do that? They shed and shit everywhere."

Daphne noticed the couple turn their heads, appalled at Britton's language, which made her smile. Britton's name was called a few minutes later, and both women went back with the nurse.

"So, you ate some bad Mexican food?" the male doctor asked, walking into the exam room.

Britton was sitting on the thin bed in the middle of the room which was surrounded by curtains.

"Yes."

"When did you eat it?" he asked, feeling her lymph nodes in her neck.

"Wednesday night."

"You're pretty dehydrated, so we're going to start an IV and give you fluids. Also, you're running a low-grade fever, so I'm going to do a blood panel to be sure we're not dealing with anything else. If everything checks out, we'll give you some nausea medicine that should help until it's out of your system."

Britton nodded.

As soon as he left the room, Daphne squeezed her hand.

"I hate needles," Britton whispered.

"I know. You'll be fine."

The nurse walked in a minute later with the fluid bag and IV kit.

"I can't believe I have to go through all of this for food poisoning," Britton scoffed as the woman prepped her arm to insert the IV.

"Oh, you'd be surprised at what people come here for. You never know if it's something else though, so we always have to take precautions, even when it's as simple as a common cold."

"That's crazy," Britton said, looking away as the woman inserted the needle and took a vial full of blood.

Daphne held Britton's other hand, reassuring her.

"Almost done," the nurse said, hooking up the fluid bag. "There you go. This will take about an hour, so by the time it's finished, your bloodwork should be back."

"Thank you." Daphne smiled.

~

An hour later, Daphne sat in the chair next to the bed, holding Britton's hand and watching the last of the fluid drip down the IV line. Britton was sound asleep. She reached over, pushing the hair away that had fallen over her cheek. The squeak of the door grabbed her attention.

"How are you feeling?" the doctor said, stepping in with her chart in his hand.

Britton stirred, slowly focusing her eyes on him as she sat up.

The doctor leaned against the foot of the bed. "You two are married to each other, correct?"

Thinking she was dealing with a homophobe, Britton's blood began to boil. "Yes! We are legally married to each other. If you have a problem with that, then you can let that door hit you on the ass on your way out!"

"Wait, wait, wait," he said, walking over and patting her shoulder. "Calm down. I don't have a problem with your marriage. My son is gay." He smiled. "I wanted to make sure before I gave you these results."

"What results?"

"Mrs. Prescott, you don't have food poisoning."

"What?" Britton said, looking slightly confused.

"You're pregnant," he said with a grin.

"What!" Daphne exclaimed.

"Are you serious?" Britton questioned. She'd been too busy cursing the Mexican place that she ate at recently to even think she could be sick because she was pregnant.

"Absolutely. The blood test is positive. I'm afraid you're dealing with a nasty bout of morning sickness."

"Oh, my God!" Daphne wrapped her arms around Britton, holding her tightly before kissing her lips.

"Holy shit," Britton murmured, still in shock.

"I take it you were expecting this?" The doctor looked from one woman to the other.

"We've been trying for months with no result, so we weren't really expecting this," Daphne replied. "We decided to get a little creative with the process this time," she said, still giddy with excitement.

"Well, it definitely worked. Let me be the first to congratulate you." He smiled. "You're fluid bag is finished, so the nurse will be here in a second to remove the IV line. You'll need to drink a lot of water and try to get some rest. Dehydration is not good at all for you or the baby."

"Baby..." Britton whispered, as she took a deep breath.

"Make sure you schedule an appointment with an obstetrician soon to follow up from this visit and keep the morning sickness under control. I've written you a prescription that should help. Don't worry, it's safe to take."

"Thank you," Daphne said, shaking his hand before he left the room. "We did it!" she giggled, squeezing Britton in another bear hug. "I love you so much!"

"I love you, too," Britton said. "I can't believe it finally worked."

"I just had a feeling that going to the cottage and letting loose would be the best time to give it a try without it weighing on our minds."

"Yeah. In all honesty, I'd kind of forgotten about it and was expecting to get my period this weekend like usual."

"No period for nine months!"

"I still can't believe it." Britton shook her head. Her entire life had changed in less than five minutes. She was still a little shocked, but also very happy. Seeing the excitement on Daphne's face and the sparkle in her eyes was well worth puking her guts out for the past twenty-four hours.

"I think we should still wait to tell people," Daphne said.

"I agree completely. We should wait until he or she is about to come out."

Daphne laughed. "You'll have a big belly at some point, so people will figure it out. You can't hide for nine months."

Britton furrowed her brow. "Well, let's at least wait until I start to show."

"That's probably a good idea." Daphne squeezed her hand.

"I hear we got some good news in this room," the nurse said, coming in to take out the IV line. "Congratulations, ladies."

"Thanks," they replied together.

They left as soon as Britton was cleared to go, walking hand-in-hand down the hall.

Chapter 24

Britton and Daphne spent the weekend cuddled together on the couch. They were overjoyed with excitement, but nervous since it was still early. They were both itching to tell everyone, so they decided to hide out in their house to avoid spilling the news. The nausea medication worked to an extent, but Britton was still puking at least twice a day. She was starting to notice certain smells that completely turned her stomach upside down.

On the way to work Monday morning, Britton called Dr. Rooney's office to make an appointment with her, which was scheduled for that Friday. She noticed a text on her phone as she pulled into the parking lot.

Good morning, did u make the appt? Daphne messaged.

Yes. Friday 9am, Britton answered as she walked towards the front door.

Ok good. Love u ☺

Love u 2, Britton replied as she stepped into her office.

"You look a little better," Kathleen said, popping her head in.

"Thanks."

"What restaurant was that? I definitely don't want to go there."

"It's actually a stomach bug, not food poisoning. The doctor told me it may last a few more days, but he gave me some medication to help with the nausea." Britton hated lying, but she and Daphne weren't ready to tell anyone. She wasn't sure it had really sunken in with her yet anyway.

"Oh, well in that case, stay away from me. I definitely don't want that either," Kathleen grimaced, backing out of the doorway.

"You can't catch it," Britton laughed to herself when her assistant was gone. She had a few phone calls and emails to return after being out sick for two days, then she headed to the back room to work on her model.

Britton noticed the strong odor of the modeling glue as soon as she opened the door. The paint-like smell immediately caused her stomach to flop. She ran to the restroom, puking up all of the minuscule breakfast she'd been able to eat.

"Damn it," she said, looking at herself in the mirror as she rinsed her mouth. "This is going to be a long fucking nine months," she muttered.

Knowing she couldn't go back into the room to work on her model as long as she could smell the glue, Britton went in search of something to impede her sense of smell. She found an old clothespin she'd used to hold something together and stuck it on her nose.

"Ouch!" she yelped, snatching it off.

Kathleen came running down the hallway. "Is everything okay?"

"Yeah. I pinched my finger with this thing."

"Ohhh, those are the heavy duty ones. I bet that hurt like hell."

"No kidding," Britton said, shaking her head. She hoped it didn't bruise.

When Kathleen went back to what she was doing, Britton Googled 'how to hide your sense of smell' on her phone. Over 100,000 links popped up. She clicked on the first one, which was written by someone who worked in a morgue. He'd said any kind of topical cream with a menthol scent works for his nose when they have a body come in that has started to decompose.

Britton closed the app on her phone and snatched her keys out of her briefcase. "I'll be right back," she yelled before walking out the front door.

She'd never been in the drugstore down the street, so Britton had to make a couple of laps around, searching up and down the aisles until she found what she was looking for. After paying the cashier, she tossed the box of Vick's VapoRub into the passenger seat and raced back to the office.

Before she walked into the back room, Britton opened the blue jar and smeared a thick line of the topical cream under her nose. The strong smell nearly caused her eyes to cross. She couldn't believe how powerful her sense of smell had gotten. She breathed through her mouth until she got used to potent menthol scent. Then, she headed into the room. The mortician had been right. Her super sniffer couldn't detect the slightest hint of the glue.

"Oh, thank God," she whispered as she sat down and began working on her model.

~

By the time lunch rolled around, Britton had reapplied the cream three times, making sure it stayed thick enough to keep her nostrils burning with menthol. Kathleen walked in to see if she wanted her to pick up lunch. She raised an eyebrow when she saw the blue jar sitting nearby and the glistening streak above Britton's top lip.

"It helps keep the nausea at bay," Britton said, noticing her odd expression.

"That stuff works wonders when you're sick. It'll even get rid of a sore throat if you eat a teaspoon of it."

"Yuck!" Britton exclaimed. "I don't think you're supposed to eat it."

Kathleen shrugged. "I'm heading out to lunch. Do you want anything?"

"No. I brought lunch today."

Kathleen stared at her like she had three heads. In the two years that she'd worked for her, Britton had never once brought her lunch in.

"I'm still having trouble keeping food down, so I brought some crackers and water." Britton smiled.

Kathleen nodded. "I sure hope you get better soon. You're getting stranger as the day goes on."

This is only the beginning, Britton thought as the door closed. "Who the hell eats topical cream?" she uttered, shivering with disgust.

~

Britton was lying on the couch with a cool rag on her forehead and a smear of Vick's under her nose when Daphne walked in.

"Hey, babe. How are you feeling?" she asked, bending down to kiss her cheek. "What the hell is on your face?"

"It's a topical cream that you rub on your chest when you're sick."

Daphne looked at her strangely.

"Apparently, being pregnant makes you have the nose of Superman. I can smell anything from a mile away and everything I pick up on makes my stomach turn. I found a website where a mortician said he uses this to cover the smell of decomposed flesh. So, I gave it a try and it works like charm."

"I see." Daphne smiled.

"It was the only way I could work because the modeling glue is so strong, I can't even go in my work room at the office."

"I didn't say anything." Daphne kissed her cheek. "What smell is bothering you here? Maybe it's something I can get rid of."

"I have no idea. I washed my face when I got home and as soon as I walked downstairs my stomach churned. I made it as far as the kitchen sink."

Daphne scrunched her face.

"So, I put it back on. I guess I'm stuck with this shit on my face for the next nine months. Oh, what fun," she scowled.

"It'll get better. I was reading about morning sickness today and I picked up this book for us while I was out at lunch."

Britton looked at the cover of the thick paperback. *What to Expect When You're Expecting* was written on the front. "Does it come with Cliff's Notes?"

Daphne laughed. "It's a long book, but it goes month by month, so you don't have to read it all at one time. From what I've read so far, the first trimester is the hardest, so once you past twelve weeks, things should get much better."

"How many weeks am I now? Two?"

"No. It starts counting back at your last cycle, I think. I'm sure Dr. Rooney will tell us how far along you are and give us the due date when we see her."

"I'm sure there's an app that tells you," Britton said, reaching for her phone.

"Britton, I'm not using a damn phone app to tell us the due date for our baby!" Daphne scolded. "We can wait until Friday."

"Fine. Pass me my crackers, please," Britton huffed.

"Do you want me to make you some soup or something?" Daphne asked, handing her the package of low sodium, saltine crackers. "Maybe you'll be able to eat it if you can't smell it."

Britton shrugged. "I don't know. I guess I'll see if it stays down."

Daphne smiled sympathetically and kissed the top of her head before walking to the kitchen.

Chapter 25

Britton and Daphne were excited and nervous when they walked into Dr. Rooney's office. They'd both been reading the book that Daphne brought home, which had definitely helped answer some of their questions, but they were happy to finally be at the doctor's office.

Britton was sitting on the exam table with Daphne standing next to her, holding her hand when Dr. Rooney walked in.

"This is a surprise!" she exclaimed.

"Yeah," they said together.

"If you don't mind my asking, how the hell did this happen?"

They both laughed. "Well," Britton started. "I decided to give it a try since she couldn't do it. We actually did it at home, using the same donor of course."

"She read about another couple who were successful with at-home artificial insemination, so we gave it a try," Daphne added.

"Wow. First time?"

"Oh, no. It took three," Britton said.

"Third time's a charm!" Dr. Rooney smiled. "Let's do a quick ultrasound to see how everything looks, then we'll figure out your due date and get you scheduled for bloodwork."

Britton nodded.

"Now, the baby is obviously extremely small, maybe about the size of a pea at this point, so we can't see it with a regular ultrasound."

Britton's eyes bugged out of her head when she saw the long, skinny wand the doctor was holding.

"This might feel a little uncomfortable, but there is no pain involved. We're just going to slid in there and take a quick peek and a couple of measurements, then we'll be all done."

Daphne rubbed her shoulder when she saw the scared look in Britton's eyes. "You'll be fine," she whispered.

Britton swallowed the lump in her throat and moved into position. Dr. Rooney eased the wand inside of her and instantly the black and white picture popped up on the screen.

"There he or she is," she said. "Would you like me to print this for you?"

"Yes!" Daphne squealed. "Oh, my God, look at that!"

"There's definitely something in there," Britton said as a tear rolled down her cheek. Reality had finally sunk in. She was going to give birth to their child. She was going to be a mother.

Daphne leaned down, kissing her cheek. "I love you so much."

"I love you, too." Britton smiled, wiping the tear before anyone noticed. "What's next for us, doc?" she asked.

Dr. Rooney removed the wand and printed the picture, before making a few notes in her chart. "When was your last cycle?"

Britton thought back, trying to remember the date.

"Do you know what day you inseminated?"

"November twenty-fifth," Daphne said.

"Are you periods regular, every twenty-eight days?" Dr. Rooney questioned.

"Yes."

"Okay, it looks like you're due date is August twentieth."

"Wow. That seems so far away," Britton said.

"It takes a while to grow a human." Dr. Rooney grinned. "Are you experiencing any issues yet?"

"I've lost eight pounds in a week because I've been extremely sick. That's actually how we found out. I thought I had food poisoning and she made me go to the ER. They prescribed a nausea medicine for me and it's helped some."

"All she's eating is saltine crackers."

"Morning sickness can be a nasty ride, but hopefully it will be over soon. You're almost five weeks along right now, so you have about seven more weeks to go before you're out of the first trimester. Morning sickness usually stops or at least slows down after that point. Make sure you're at least trying to eat. Even if it comes up, you're body is holding onto nutrients. Also, drink a lot of water and get started on a prenatal vitamin if you haven't already."

"I started those last weekend," Britton said.

"Great. Do you have any questions for me?"

Britton and Daphne looked at each other, then shook their heads.

"Well, you have my number. Give me a call if you need to. Otherwise, I'll see you back here in six weeks. Remember, your body is rapidly changing, so make sure you get a lot of rest and try to eat nutritious food. You can supplement the crackers if you need to so that you at least have something in your stomach."

"Okay," Britton replied, shaking her hand.

"Merry Christmas, ladies."

"Yeah, no kidding," they laughed.

"August seems like forever," Daphne murmured as the doctor left the room. She was holding the black and white print out of their little bean.

"Hopefully it goes by fast." Britton took the paper gown off and began getting dressed.

Chapter 26

The first snowfall of the season blanketed their area a couple days before Christmas. Britton walked inside her house after a long day at the office. The model was slowly coming together, and she was still battling morning sickness, throwing up at least once a day. She'd lost nearly fifteen pounds from not being able to keep much food down, and she'd quit going to the gym, which made her start to lose muscle mass. The rapid weight loss was obvious in her loose clothes and starting to show more on her face.

"You have snow in your hair," Daphne said, wiping away the flurries.

"It was just starting to get thicker when I left work."

"That's why I left a little early. I didn't want to drive in that mess in the dark." She wrapped her arms around Britton, kissing her lips. "How are you feeling?"

"A little hungry."

"That's a good sign." Daphne smiled.

"Not really. I was starving this morning, so I made an egg white omelet with veggies in it." Britton shook her head. "That did not taste as good coming back up."

"Aww…" Daphne hugged her tightly, running her hands up and down her back. "Do you want to try some

157

chicken and rice with a little bit of veggies? I made it pretty bland for you."

"I guess." Britton pulled away, looking out the window in the formal living room. "Look how bad it's coming down now."

"Yeah, I'm glad we got all of our shopping done early this year."

"I was hoping we could ride around and look at Christmas lights tonight," Britton sighed.

"Why don't we try for tomorrow night?"

"That sounds like a good idea," Britton said, sitting down at the table with Daphne. She started with slow bites of her dinner, hoping it stayed down. "How am I going to eat at your parent's house Christmas Eve and mine Christmas Day?" she sighed.

"Just do a little at a time and hopefully you can keep it down," Daphne said reassuringly.

"I can't believe how much weight I've lost. None of my clothes fit."

"Look at it this way, when you finally do start gaining, it won't be as much as a lot of people because you have a huge deficit to make up."

"Once I get over being sick, I'm going to start going back to the gym. I can walk on the treadmill and use the elliptical machine, at least until I can't see my feet or get uncomfortable. I don't want to gain fifty pounds."

"You probably won't. Most women gain about thirty pounds according to that book. As long as you eat healthy food and exercise as long as you can, you won't get huge."

"I hope so."

~

Christmas Eve went by quickly. Britton and Daphne had dinner with Daphne's parents, which Britton pretty much pushed around her plate to make it look like she'd eaten, then they exchanged a few gifts. By the time they'd left, Britton was exhausted and fell asleep on the ride home.

The next morning, Daphne awoke alone. The space next to her in the bed was cool, indicating Britton had been up for some time. She pulled on her robe to ward off the chill in the air, and padded down the stairs, looking for her wife.

"Good morning," Britton said, kissing her softly when Daphne found her in the kitchen.

The smell of coffee tickled Daphne's nose and she quickly poured herself a cup. "How long have you been up?" she asked.

"Oh, I don't know. A half hour, maybe."

"I can't believe you still get up early like a little kid on Christmas morning. I think Santa quit making stops at your house a long time ago." Daphne smiled.

"Actually, he came here last night," Britton said nonchalantly.

"What?"

"He left you something by the tree."

Daphne set her mug on the counter and walked into their formal living room. A dozen or so presents were all wrapped in the same paper under the tree. Those were from Britton and Daphne to each other, as well as to Britton's family and Heather and Greg. However, a box wrapped in shiny red paper with green ribbon and a big green bow was sitting off to the side. The tag read:

Graysen Morgen

To: Daphne
From: Santa

Daphne furrowed her brow as she sat down on the sofa and tore open the paper. Under the paper was a thin white box, which she then opened. Inside, she found an eight by ten frame with a large photo across the top of the beach cottage in White Hill. Underneath that was two smaller pictures side by side. One was of the two of them at their elopement on the beach there, and the other was the ultrasound picture of the baby in the shape of a tiny pea.

"Britton, this is beautiful."

"That's where we started our life together and where we created a life together. I figured it needed to officially be ours."

"What do you mean?"

"Keep looking in the box."

Daphne pulled the frame completely out and found an envelope under it.

"That's the deed. We now own the Seaside Cottage. Merry Christmas," Britton said with a huge smile.

"Britton!" Daphne rushed into her arms. "Oh, my God!"

"I love you and I know how much that place means to both of us. It's ours forever."

"I love you, too. This is the best gift ever…well, next to this of course," she said, rubbing Britton's belly. "How did you get them to sell it?"

"I took this photo down and told them we made our baby in there and after also getting married right in front of it on that beach, it would mean the world to us to have in our family. They were a little hesitant, but then I called the old man, who is doing much better by the way. He took my offer and I went down there to sign the papers. We actually closed on it two days ago, which is why I was so late getting home. I got stuck in traffic."

Daphne nodded. "You amaze me. Every time I think how lucky I am to have you in my life, you blow my mind with something new. I never thought I could love someone as much as I love you. I'm so glad I get to spend the rest of my life with you, Britton. You're everything to me."

"I feel the same way. You've completely changed my life, Daphne. This is an adventure I never want to end and a ride I never want to get off of."

Daphne ran her hands down the front of Britton's chest as she leaned in, kissing her passionately. Britton pulled away.

"What's wrong?" Daphne asked.

"You taste like coffee," Britton scrunched her face as she stomach rolled.

"Are you going to be sick?"

"I think I'm okay," she said, sitting down.

"I'll be glad when you're past this point," Daphne sighed.

"Me too." Britton looked at the rest of the gifts under the tree. "So, what did you get me?" she asked, sounding like a little kid.

"Certainly not a beachfront cottage," Daphne laughed, handing her a couple of packages to open.

Britton grinned as she tore into them. The first present was a gold watch with a black face and diamonds in the place of numbers.

"I love it!" Britton exclaimed, quickly putting it on. "I'd kiss you but…"

Daphne rolled her eyes. "Let me finish this cup and I'll go brush my teeth."

Chapter 27

Britton and Daphne arrived at Britton's parents' house just before noon. Bridget and Wade were running a little late after seeing his parents earlier that morning.

"Merry Christmas," Sharon Prescott said, hugging Daphne. She gasped when she saw Britton. "What's going on?" she questioned.

"What do you mean?" Britton stepped forward, hugging her mother.

"You're skin and bones, Britton Marie. Are you sick? What are you not telling me?" Sharon was used to seeing her daughter's slender, muscular figure. She'd always been built like an athlete, from years of elite rowing.

"I'm fine, mother. I've been a little stressed lately and I haven't been going to the gym. I've lost a little weight."

"A little!"

"What's all the commotion? Merry Christmas, Daphne," Stephen Prescott said, walking up and hugging her.

"Look at your daughter," Sharon said.

He raised an eyebrow. "Are you sick?"

"No, Daddy. I quit going to the gym, so I've lost weight. I'm fine."

"Are you okay with her looking like this?" Sharon asked Daphne.

"It's not forever. She's been busy and under a lot of stress. After a couple of months, she'll be back to normal." Daphne smiled.

Britton's father ushered everyone through the family room where a huge Christmas tree was decorated with presents under it, and out to the solarium. Daphne added the presents they'd brought to the small pile as she passed by. As soon as she sat down next to Britton at the table, the doorbell rang. Britton stared around at the mass of food on display with her stomach flip flopping around as she waited for her parents to return with Bridget and Wade.

"Merry Christmas," Bridget said, coming around to hug her best friend first, then her sister.

Daphne and Britton stood.

"Wow, you've lost a lot of weight. Are you okay?" Bridget asked, hugging her sister.

"Yes. Everything is good."

"I'm surprised to see you two here together," Sharon said to Bridget. "Given the circumstances and all."

"Mom, Wade and I are not getting divorced," Bridget said.

"Well, whatever is going on, we are okay with it. There's no need to be embarrassed or ashamed to talk to us."

"Bridget and Wade aren't ready to have kids because she's too busy preparing to take Daddy's place with the company, which is what she's been drilled to do since we were teenagers!" Britton lashed out. "I didn't want the job, so she had to step up and be the one to do it, despite knowing that you wanted me in that position all along. If you sat back and looked at Bridget, you'd see how hard she is working for this family's business. A kid simply doesn't fit in with her life at the moment. Bridget and Wade are happy and damn it, when they chose to have a kid, it will be their decision. Not yours or anyone else's!" Britton's blood pressure had gone way up and she was light-headed.

Britton's mother and her sister both sat there, shocked.

"How dare you come into this house and speak to your mother this way. We didn't raise you to be this disrespectful!" her father yelled.

Britton tried to calm herself down, but her blood was racing and her stomach was rolling back and forth. As her mother began to say something, she jumped up from the table and rushed out the side door since she was too far from the restroom inside the house. Daphne took off behind her, holding Britton's hair as she puked in the snow.

Everyone was staring at them when they turned around. Britton squished some fresh snow around her mouth and spit it out, rinsing the acidic taste before Daphne held her up.

"Call an ambulance," Stephen yelled to the maid.

"I'm fine," Britton said. "I'm sorry for yelling, but—"

"You look pale and you're running a fever," her mother said, frantically looking over her and touching her forehead. "What is wrong with you?"

Bridget went to her other side, opposite of Daphne. "Are you sure? You don't look well at all, Britt. Daphne, what's going on?"

"Celine! Where's the ambulance?" Stephen shouted to the maid.

"Everyone calm down!" Britton yelled, backing away from all of them. "We don't need an ambulance."

"Well, you need to go to the hospital or something," Bridget said. "How long have you been sick?"

"I'm not sick...I'm pregnant," Britton blurted out.

"What?" Sharon and Bridget gasped together.

"Since when?" Stephen asked.

"Why didn't you tell me?" Sharon asked her daughter.

Bridget looked at Daphne. "I'd like to ask you the same thing. Why didn't you guys tell anyone?"

"We didn't say anything because we wanted to do this on our own. It's been a long, difficult process and we didn't want anyone else involved," Britton replied.

"Why are you so sick and skinny looking?" Bridget asked.

"I've been battling severe morning sickness and not working out every day, so I've lost about fifteen pounds. I'm fine. The doctor said everything looks good."

"I'm going to be a grandmother!" Sharon exclaimed, hugging Daphne and Britton. "I can't believe this! How in the world did this happen?"

"I don't think you want the details," Bridget laughed.

"Well, no." Her mother shook her head as Wade congratulated them.

"Actually, we tried for months with Daphne, but she has a condition that won't allow her to get pregnant. So, I decided to have our baby."

"Oh, Daph. Why didn't you tell me?" Bridget wrapped her arms around her best friend.

"We wanted to do this ourselves. It's been a long road, but we couldn't be happier."

"I'm proud of you and happy for you both," Stephen said, hugging his daughter.

"Thanks, Daddy. What do you think about being a grandpa?"

He shrugged and smiled. "I have no idea."

"Yeah, it takes a little bit for it to sink in," she replied. "I think Mom's a little further into the game than you are."

"How far along are you, Britt?" her sister asked.

"Six weeks. I'm due in August."

"A summer baby, how exciting!" Sharon exclaimed as she went to get some champagne to celebrate.

"You're in for it now," Bridget whispered.

"I know. She's going to try to take over my life," Britton said.

"Hey, better you than me. At least now I won't be getting divorced every month," Bridget laughed. "I really am happy for you both. I wish you had told me…about everything," she said to Daphne.

"It was so hard not to. I even picked up the phone a few times, but Britton is my wife and we leaned on each other, which is what you do when you're married. I love her with everything that I am, Bridge. She's my whole world."

"I know. I see it every time you look at each other." She smiled, squeezing Daphne's hand. "I'm going to be an aunt!" she cheered.

Later that evening, Britton was completely exhausted and nearly passed out on the couch in the den. Daphne was sitting on the end, with Britton's feet in her lap, softly massaging them as they watched a cheesy holiday movie.

"I need to tell Heather," Britton mumbled. "I guess we can do it tomorrow night at dinner."

"Yeah, I need to tell my parents first. Otherwise, when Heather tells her mother, my aunt will surely call my mom. I guess I'll do it now," Daphne said. "I should've told them last night. I hate doing it over the phone."

"We weren't telling anyone for another couple of months, but I had to do something. My family was freaking out."

"I know."

"Why don't you call and invite them over for lunch tomorrow? We can tell them then," Britton suggested.

"That's a great idea." Daphne got up to make the call. When she returned a few minutes later, Britton was sound asleep.

Chapter 28

The next evening, Britton and Daphne went over to Heather and Greg's to exchange gifts and have dinner. More snow had fallen, making them late.

"I was wondering if you were going to show up," Heather said, opening the door.

"We got a little sidetracked," Britton replied, wiggling her eyebrows.

"Don't lie to her," Daphne chided. "Britton fell asleep after my parents left and woke up grumpy."

Britton shook her head and went to go hang her jacket up and give Greg a hug.

"How was lunch?" Heather asked.

"Good. You know how my parents are. My mother can't just accept things, she has to come to terms with them."

"She's not still questioning your relationship, is she?"

"Oh, no. She stopped doing that after we got married. She's just…you know how mothers are. They think they know everything."

"Yeah, no kidding," Heather replied, opening the wine cooler in the dining room. "What do you think, red or white?"

"Well…" Daphne looked around for Britton.

Graysen Morgen

"We're having Italian. I don't want to see or eat turkey meat until after Easter." Heather grinned.

"What's going on?" Britton asked, walking up behind Daphne and sliding her arms around her waist.

"We're trying to decide on the wine," Daphne said.

Britton stepped around Daphne and grabbed one of the chardonnay bottles. "This should go well with Manicotti. That is what you made, isn't it?"

Heather raised an eyebrow. "How did you know?"

"I smelled it when we walked in."

Daphne shook her head and laughed.

"What's going on with you?" Heather asked, finally noticing how gaunt her best friend looked since she'd removed her winter coat. "You look like you're anorexic or something. Are you okay?"

"Actually, there's something we need to tell you guys," Britton said.

"Oh, my God...are you sick?" Heather nearly dropped the bottle of wine.

"No. I'm fine." Britton grabbed her hand and pulled her into the living room where Greg was watching TV.

Heather pressed the mute button on the nearby controller, causing Greg to huff like a little kid. Heather gave him a stern look and nodded towards Britton.

Britton grabbed Daphne's hand and smiled at her. "I'm pregnant," she said.

"What?" Heather's jaw hit the floor. "Are you serious?"

Britton and Daphne nodded.

"How the hell did that happen?" Greg questioned. Heather smacked him on the arm.

"Want me to show you?" Britton laughed. "Bend over!"

"Wow! I can't believe this. No wonder you've been avoiding me. I mean, I know married life changes people, but I've barely seen you in the last six months."

"I know. I'm sorry. We've been through hell. When we decided to have a baby, Daphne wanted to give birth. We went through month after month of letdowns and we didn't want our family and friends involved. It was difficult enough for us as it was. When we found out she couldn't conceive, I decided to carry."

"Aww," Heather said, hugging her cousin and then her best friend as a few tears slipped down her cheeks. "I'm sad and happy for you both. This is amazing."

"Congratulations," Greg said, hugging them.

"I still can't believe you're pregnant," Heather said. "Why have you lost so much weight? Shouldn't you be gaining?"

"I've been extremely ill with morning sickness."

"Oh, you poor thing. That sucks. What did the doctor say?"

"She put me on medication that helps with the nausea, but my nose is working on overdrive, so I can just about smell China from here. Every other scent turns my stomach, as does most food."

"I've heard about that."

"It should pass when she's out of her first trimester though,," Daphne added.

"How far along are you?"

"Only six weeks. We hadn't planned to tell anyone for a couple more months, but my mother pissed me off and I lost it on her, which turned into a fiasco and I blurted it out," Britton said.

Heather laughed. "I bet your mother was floored."

"We pretty much had to scrape her off the ceiling, she was so excited. But at first, yeah everyone was shocked. We did it yesterday."

"Wow. So, Bridget and Wade were there?"

"Yes. That's what upset me. My mother went on like they were getting divorced right in front of them. I couldn't take it anymore. You know my sister has no backbone when it comes to our parents. I had to stand up for her."

"You definitely did that," Daphne giggled.

"Was it bad?" Heather asked.

"No. She told it like it was, but then she got herself all worked up and puked her guts out. Her dad flipped out, trying to call 9-1-1, so she had to tell them."

Heather laughed hysterically. "Oh, I wish I could've seen that."

"It's funny now," Britton chuckled. "But at the time, it was life or death at the dinner table."

"What about your parents?" Heather asked Daphne. "I'm sure they were shocked."

"That's putting it mildly. My mother had more questions about the donor, who is completely unknown and will remain that way," Daphne replied.

"That's crazy. It's no one's business. You two are married and you're having a baby together. It's not rocket science to figure out you needed to get sperm from somewhere." Heather shook her head. "I love you, Daph, but your mother is a flake sometimes."

"Trust me, I know."

"What did she say about you and all of that?"

"Not much. I didn't go into major details. I only said I'd tried for months with the doctor and was unable to get pregnant."

"I'm sorry you guys went through all of that. I wish you would've told me," she said to Britton.

"I wanted to, but we had to do this together."

"For once, I knew something before you did," Daphne joked with her cousin.

"I doubt that. You two are like spaghetti and sauce. Once you got together, there was no separating you," Heather laughed. "Speaking of Italian food…dinner is ready."

"Hey, Britt, I guess now you have to get rid of that race car you drive," Greg said.

"What? No one mentioned anything about that."

"Where are you going to put the baby's car seat?" Heather questioned.

"Next to me in the passenger seat, of course."

Heather shook her head. "That's against the law."

"Oh, bullshit."

"It is," Daphne muttered.

"Come on!" Britton growled. "I have eight more months to figure it out."

"Technically thirty-four weeks," Daphne mumbled.

Britton shot her a look and crossed her arms in defiance.

Chapter 29

Daphne spent New Year's Eve in front of the TV, watching the ball drop in Times Square. Britton had fallen asleep around eleven, stretched out on the couch with her head in Daphne's lap and the *What to Expect When You're Expecting* book lying open on her chest. Daphne closed the book and ran her fingers slowly through Britton's shoulder-length locks.

"Happy New Year," she whispered, kissing her fingers and placing them on Britton's cheek.

~

Two weeks later, the mayor finally found time in his schedule to meet with Britton. She completely blew his mind with her model presentation. Seeing the vast detail of the sketches come to life in the form of a scaled 3D model was amazing.

"This is going to be centerpiece for downtown Providence," he declared with a big grin.

Britton smiled.

"Honestly, I went into this meeting not knowing what to expect. Your initial sketches were above and beyond anything anyone else presented, so much so, that I wasn't sure you'd be able to pull off your own idea, but you've proven me wrong, once again. I only hope the builder is half as good as you are."

"I actually met with them yesterday to go over the model. They're as excited as we are about this project. This is the type of construction they do. Their work is phenomenal."

"Yeah, I saw the pictures you emailed me. I'm looking forward to getting started. The permits should be ready with the next week, so we're planning the groundbreaking ceremony for the week after."

"Sounds good," she replied, shaking his hand. Kissing his ass wasn't at the top of her list, but this project was huge and had the potential to put her name on the map as one of the top architects in the country.

"Would you like to have lunch? I have a table a Grogan's," he said, mentioning one of the city's five-star steakhouses.

"I'd love to, but I actually already have lunch plans." She smiled. "I'll touch base with you next week regarding the permits."

Britton checked her watch as she walked out of the City Hall building. She was already five minutes late.

~

Heather munched on an appetizer, shaking her head when she saw her best friend rush inside the restaurant and slid into the opposite side of the booth.

"I'm sorry. Mayor Ass Napkin wouldn't stop talking." She shook her head and sipped her water.

"Did he approve everything?" Heather asked.

"Oh, yeah. We're waiting on the permits now. We'll probably break ground in about two weeks."

"That's good. How have you been feeling?"

"Like shit," Britton answered honestly. "I'm still puking every day, but I'm eating a lot of small meals to keep my strength up. I'm so tired I literally pass out on the couch every night."

"Well, your body is working overtime building a little human. You have to take it easy."

"You sound like Daphne," Britton said, pausing to order a bowl of chicken noodle soup and a house salad. "I think the morning sickness is what is exhausting me. I'm nauseated twenty-four-seven."

"Hopefully that will go away soon."

"I only have three more weeks until I'm out of the first trimester, thank God. It's literally been hell. I don't know how women do this over and over."

"Do you think you'll do it again?" Heather asked.

Britton raised an eyebrow and shook her head. "Thankfully, Daphne and I decided this is it. We went through so much to get this one child, I couldn't imagine ever going through it again."

Heather nodded. "It's definitely not for everyone, that's for sure. I don't know how women have a pile of kids either. I guess if you want a big family, you're prepared for that."

When the waiter brought their food, Britton ate a little of the soup and picked around the salad until her stomach had had enough.

"You really aren't eating much," Heather said.

"Nope. A little here, a little there. I keep about fifty percent of it down throughout the day."

"That sounds so unappealing. I don't ever want to get pregnant," Heather laughed.

"I never in my life thought I'd be sitting here nearly three months pregnant, but as miserable as I am, I wouldn't change it."

"You and Daphne are the epitome of the perfect couple."

"Oh, please. We're just like everyone else, we just happen to be the same sex."

"I don't think in the three years you've been together that you've ever fought, have you?"

"Of course, but it's usually a simple argument over stupid shit. You and Greg don't have huge knockdown, drag-out fights, do you?"

"Well, no. He acts like a big kid sometimes, but all men do." Heather rolled her eyes.

"See, you need to have a child so he'll have a playmate," Britton teased.

"Not anytime soon, thank you. A baby is definitely not something we are ready for." She pushed her plate aside and reached for the bill. Britton tried to take it from her, but she wouldn't allow it. "I invited you, remember?"

"Next one's on me then."

"So, what do you guys want more, a boy or girl?"

Britton shrugged. "We honestly don't care. Personally, I'd be happy with either one. I think my dad wants a grandson so bad he can taste it. My mom hasn't said much either way, but I'm sure she wants a little girl to dress up and show off."

"That's going to be one spoiled rotten kid," Heather laughed.

"No kidding. I'm going to have to lay down some ground rules with the two of them before it's even born."

"Has your mom begun planning the shower yet?" Heather giggled.

"No! I told her not to mention that word to me for another three months at least. Daphne's mom mentioned having a shower of her own though."

"My aunt is so damn weird." Heather shook her head as she stood up. "My mom is really excited for you guys though."

"Tell her I said hi." Britton stood and followed her outside, giving her a quick hug before walking to her own car.

"Enjoy that ride while you can," Heather teased.

Britton shot her a bird and grinned as she got in and raced out of the parking lot.

Chapter 30

Britton was happy to see her twelfth week roll around. The first trimester had been a long, hard-fought battle, but she'd prevailed. Walking into Dr. Rooney's office, she felt a little excited about moving to the next stage. The nurse who took them back to the exam room couldn't keep her eyes off Daphne, which didn't go unnoticed by Britton.

"She must be new," Britton growled as she left the room.

"What's wrong?" Daphne asked.

The woman walked back into the room and put her hand on Daphne's shoulder. "Pardon me for a second," she said as she put the blood pressure cuff on Britton and pressed the button to start the machine.

Britton stared daggers at her.

"So, is this your sister?" the woman asked, looking at Daphne. She obviously hadn't looked in Britton's chart.

"Actually," Britton said, reaching over and putting their left hands together. "She is my wife."

The nurse nodded and rolled the blood pressure machine out of the way before leaving the room without saying another word.

"I'd smack her if I wasn't pregnant," Britton sneered.

"Calm down." Daphne smiled, rubbing her forearm.

Dr. Rooney walked in a few minutes later. "How are we doing this morning, ladies?" she said, opening Britton's chart. "Your blood pressure is a little high."

"That's because your nurse just tried to pick up my wife," Britton muttered.

Dr. Rooney raised an eyebrow. "Seriously?"

Daphne shrugged. "It's not a big deal."

"I'll say something if you want."

"No. It's fine. Britton isn't feeling too good this morning," Daphne replied.

"Are you still battling morning sickness?"

"A little nausea here and there, but I haven't puked in a few days."

"You've lost quite a bit of weight, but it should start to return soon, especially if you're keeping more food down. Morning sickness usually goes away between weeks twelve and fourteen." Dr. Rooney set the chart aside pushed Britton's shirt up, revealing her abdomen, which was still flat. "Let's see what your little peanut is up to." She squirted a dot of gel under her belly button and placed the ultrasound probe in it.

Britton and Daphne watched the screen as Dr. Rooney moved the probe around her belly.

"Here it is. Everything looks great," Dr. Rooney said, taking measurements and entering them into the computer.

"It's so little!" Daphne exclaimed.

"Look, it's moving around!" Britton added with a big smile.

Dr. Rooney turned on the volume, allowing Britton and Daphne to hear their baby's heartbeat for the first time. Daphne squeezed Britton's hand as both women wiped away tears.

"Oh, my God," Britton whispered.

"That's amazing. I'm so proud of you," Daphne murmured.

Dr. Rooney printed them a couple of new pictures, then turned everything off. She handed Britton a paper towel to wipe away the gel. "Everything looks great, ladies. I'll see you back here in four weeks."

Britton nodded and shook the doctor's hand while Daphne stared at the black and white pictures she was holding.

"That's our baby," Britton said, kissing her cheek.

"This is the most incredible thing I've ever seen. Knowing there is little person inside of you, moving all around, is so surreal."

"Yeah. I never imagined it myself either, but we did it. Our love made that little person."

Daphne wrapped her arms around Britton's neck and Britton held her tight.

~

Two weeks later, the nausea had finally subsided enough for Britton to eat full meals. Valentine's Day had come and gone with a simple dinner at home. Despite losing so much weight, her belly was no longer flat. It had finally begun to round and stick out about an inch past the waistband of her pants. She found that as much as she disliked the fit and look of most maternity pants, they were more comfortable and fit better than the tighter slacks she normally wore. She'd also had to tell Kathleen that she was pregnant since it was becoming more noticeable. Of course, she was ecstatic and promised not to act like a mother hen.

The groundbreaking ceremony for the art museum had gone off without a hitch and the builders had finally begun construction, which was a huge sigh of relief for Britton. This was more than likely going to be her last big project until after the baby was born. She'd put a bid in for a new school over in Pawtucket, but she hadn't heard anything and Senator Ferguson was battling with his wife over whether or not to add a guest house to the cottage. The stress of making sure the museum came together without any hiccups was enough. She didn't need any added anxiety.

~

On the last day of her fourth month of pregnancy, Britton was sitting at her desk, feeling exhausted from a long work week, when her cell phone lit up with Heather's picture.

"Hey," Britton answered cheerfully.

"Are you busy?" Heather stammered.

"Not really. What's up?"

"Can you meet me...now?" Heather sounded a little more frantic.

"Yes. Is everything okay?"

"No," Heather murmured.

"Are you at home? I'm on the way." Britton grabbed her briefcase and headed out of her office.

"Yes," Heather replied softly before hanging up.

Unsure what was going on, Britton drove as fast as she could, while still being safe. She couldn't put herself or her unborn child in danger on the busy streets.

Pulling into Heather's driveway fifteen minutes later, she got out and hurried inside. Heather was sitting on the couch with her head in her hands.

"Honey, what's going on?" Britton asked, sitting down next to her and rubbing her back to console her. "Did Greg do something stupid?"

"I'm pregnant," Heather cried.

"No shit?" Britton exclaimed.

"No shit," Heather pouted. "We aren't ready for this. I have no idea how to tell Greg."

"I take it you just found out."

"Yeah. I went to the doctor for my annual visit and you know how they always do a urine test, well it came back positive. I didn't believe it, so she did an ultrasound. I'm about eight weeks. Britton, I had no idea. My periods have never been normal, so missing one here or there is not unusual for me. I haven't been sick or anything."

"Wow." Britton held her best friend. "Heather, this should be exciting for you, not sad. I know you guys weren't ready, but most straight couples aren't. It just happens. You're married and you love each other. What more do you need?"

"To go back eight weeks ago and pretend to have a headache," she sighed, shaking her head. "When you told us you were pregnant we both said that wasn't what we wanted right now. We had this grand idea to wait another year and see where we are."

"Everything happens for a reason, honey."

"What is Greg going to say? This is going to be the ultimate test for our marriage."

"Stop beating yourself up. Greg is your husband, not some guy you've been dating for a few weeks. Cut him some slack. Yes, you guys had an accident, but Heather, that's how most kids are conceived. You'll get through this."

"You're right. My mind is all over the place."

"You should be happy right now, especially because you didn't get sick for three whole months, you bitch," Britton teased.

Heather laughed.

"The fuzzy head you're experiencing is called pregnancy brain. It gets worse. I forget shit all the time and it drives me nuts."

"Great." Heather smiled. "I have no idea what to do next."

"I'm sure your doctor talked to you."

"Yeah, but I was in shock. I don't remember much of what she said."

"Go get prenatal vitamins. That should be your first step, then pick up a copy of *What to Expect When You're Expecting*. That book is a godsend. But, above all else, tell your husband he's going to be a father."

"Wow, when you put it like that, it definitely sinks in."

"A bottle of wine sounds good right about now, huh?" Britton grinned and they both laughed as she got up to go to the restroom.

"I never in a million years thought we'd be sitting here both pregnant," Heather stated when Britton returned.

"Me either, that's for damn sure. But, here we are." Britton smiled.

Look at your belly," Heather said, noticing the protrusion for the first time. She reached over, rubbing her hand across the roundness. "It's so cute."

Britton laughed. "Yeah, we'll see how cute it is when I can't see my damn feet." Her belly was hard and round, but still fairly small for someone almost five months pregnant.

"I'm not looking forward to that either," Heather giggled as she watched her get up again. "Where are you going?"

"To pee."

"You just went," Heather said.

"That's something else you have to look forward to. This little shit is stomping on my bladder. I have to pee every ten minutes." Britton smirked sarcastically as she walked down the hall.

When Britton returned, she said, "You know I'm going to tell Daphne, she's my wife and we don't keep secrets, but I'll make sure she doesn't tell her mother."

"Thanks. I don't care if she knows, or your family for that matter. I'm going to tell Greg tonight and I guess we'll tell our families tomorrow since the weekend is here."

"Let me know how it goes. You'll be fine. You guys love each other and your mother is going to be over the moon."

"That's certainly true." Heather stood and hugged her best friend. "I don't know what I'd do without you in my life."

"I feel the same way," Britton said, patting her shoulder. "It'll all work out and the next time I see you, we'll both be fat."

Heather rolled her eyes and laughed.

Chapter 31

Britton was sitting on the couch with her feet propped up on the table, sketching a building from the paused picture on the TV when Daphne walked in.

"You haven't done that in a while," Daphne said, kissing her cheek.

"I've been too damn busy to do much of anything, between designing buildings and making babies, there hasn't been a lot of *me* time. How was your day?"

"Good. I'm glad it's Friday," Daphne replied, sitting down next to her.

"Me too."

"You must've come home early," she murmured, looking at the drawing on the pad in Britton's lap.

"Yeah, about two hours ago. I had to go over to Heather's earlier and I decided just to come home afterwards."

"Why were you at Heather's?" Daphne questioned. "Was she off today?"

"Yes. She went for her annual probing."

"Uh, that's no fun."

"Oh, it gets better," Britton added, still drawing.

Daphne raised an eyebrow.

"She's pregnant," Britton said with her eyes glued to her paper.

"Get out. Are you serious?"

"Yep. Eight weeks along. She's always had irregular periods so she had no idea."

"Wow! What did Greg say? I take it they weren't planning this."

"Nope. She hasn't told him yet. She called me in a frenzied mess. I had to go calm her down. She's fine now. She's telling him tonight. Don't say anything to your parents."

"I won't. I'm sure my aunt is going to be happy." Daphne leaned back against the cushions. "That's crazy."

"It definitely took her by surprise, that's for sure." Britton finished the last part of her drawing and set the pad aside. "That bitch never puked once," she pouted.

Daphne laughed and patted her thigh before putting her hand on Britton's little round belly. "I was thinking of checking out that new baby store tomorrow," she said.

"The one at Market Square?"

"Yeah."

Britton shrugged. "Sure."

Daphne kissed her lips softly. "What do you want for dinner?"

"I have a bad craving for a giant bowl of spaghetti and meatballs." Britton grinned sheepishly.

"I'll call in a takeout order from Maria's," Daphne laughed. "You're definitely feeling better."

~

On the way to the store the next morning, Daphne casually swung into the Porsche dealer.

"What are we doing here?" Britton asked.

"You need a new car."

"Says who?"

"Britton, you drive a two-seater sports car and we're having a baby," Daphne sighed. "I'm not saying you have to do anything today, but at least look around."

"Fine," Britton groaned, getting out of the car. She knew Daphne was right, but she wasn't ready to part with her car. It had cost her a fortune and she loved every minute of driving it.

Daphne lagged back as Britton looked around. Every time a salesman approached, she shook her head, knowing her wife all too well. When Britton was ready, she'd come home with a new car and it would be the exact car she wanted, not something a salesman tried to talk her into. This was only a little push from Daphne in that direction, before they eventually ran out of time.

Thirty minutes later, Britton had examined each and every four-door car on the showroom floor and walked away with a few brochures.

"Did you see anything you like?" Daphne asked as they walked back out to her car.

"I don't know." Britton shrugged.

Daphne sighed as she drove towards the baby store a few blocks away.

~

After a long afternoon, they finally made it back home, bringing a catalog from the baby store and brochures from two different furniture stores with him.

"I guess we should start talking about the nursery," Britton said, sitting down on the couch. "All of the spare rooms are on the opposite side of the house. I guess I didn't really think about having to go back and forth to a baby's room when I designed this place. I was thinking more long-term when the kids were older and we wanted privacy."

Daphne sat down next to her and opened the catalog for the baby store. "He or she will be in our room for the first few months in a bassinet. After that, we'll be able to move him or her to the crib and we'll get one of those video monitors so we can see everything. So, it probably won't matter what room we choose."

"How about the middle room? It's already a sky blue color with white trim. I think a boy or girl would be happy with that. Since we are going with a unisex theme anyway, we won't have to repaint it."

"That's true. I like that one. Speaking of the theme, we need to decide on one. We only have about two months before everyone is going to be hounding us about a shower. I think we should definitely have the registry completed before then."

"I agree," Britton replied, looking through the pages with her. "There's a lot of shit here."

"Yep. We're going to need all of this shit, too." Daphne smiled.

"Maybe we should choose a bigger room."

Daphne laughed. "That middle room is plenty big. It's twice the size of the room I had as a kid. We didn't all grow up in an estate house."

"My parents didn't move into the estate house until I was eighteen."

"I know that, but the house you lived in when we were in high school was still huge compared to my parents' house."

"I guess it was about the size of this one."

"Exactly." Daphne grinned.

"Did I tell you my mom is convinced we're having a girl?" Britton said, changing the subject.

"No. Why does she think that?"

"Old wives tales or some crazy shit. She was sick with both me and my sister, so because I had severe morning sickness, it's most definitely a girl."

"I guess we'll see when he or she comes out. Speaking of that, my mom thinks we need to find out the sex and not wait. I tried to explain to her that we don't care either way, so we are excited about the surprise."

"Maybe we should move away...really far away," Britton murmured.

Daphne chuckled. "They'd probably all follow us."

"Not if we go to the jungle."

"So, you want to live like Tarzan and Jane?" Daphne raised an eyebrow.

"You can wear a loin cloth once in a while. I won't mind." Britton shrugged.

"You're a mess," Daphne laughed. "Hey, speaking of the jungle, that's not a bad idea for a theme."

"You want to make the room full of vines and wild animals?"

"Not exactly, but animals aren't a bad idea, or even one type of animal in particular like monkeys."

"If you put monkeys all over the room, he or she is going to grow up hating them," Britton retorted. "I was thinking maybe letters and numbers or something along those lines."

"That's boring."

"Okay, well I think loud colors are a bad idea. All of these unisex bedding sets are ugly," Britton said, flipping through the pages in the catalog. Looking at a few different ones gave her an idea. "I'll be right back."

Daphne pursed her lips as she watched her walk away and return a minute later with her sketch pad and pencil set. She kept looking through the catalog as Britton began drawing something.

"What do you think about something like this?" Britton asked. "The room is already sky blue, so we could paint some gray trees and teal colored animals like maybe a monkey and a giraffe, and we could also add in yellow butterflies or birds. This gives us neutral colors and a unisex theme."

"That's a neat idea," Daphne exclaimed. "I think I saw a bedding set that would go with that." She went back a few pages. "Here it is."

Britton looked at the picture of the quilt which was white, but had large squares with a different light gray pattern in each one. "I like this idea with only gray and white. Then, the art we put on the walls will add color to the room, but it won't be overpowering."

Daphne drew a big circle around the bedding set. "Great. Now, we need a furniture set. What color do you think?"

"I think dark furniture will stick out too much," Britton said.

"I agree. We can go with honey or another shade of brown."

"What about white?"

"I didn't think of that. White will probably look the best." Daphne nodded, opening the brochures from the furniture stores.

Chapter 32

Two weeks later, they finally decided on a furniture collection and gave away the bed and dresser set that had been in the now-nursery. Once the room was empty, Britton began sketching the trees and animal designs on the walls. She left a large open space to add in the babies name after he or she was born.

"I should be finished with the pattern on the nursery walls this weekend," Britton said as they walked into Dr. Rooney's office. "I can't believe it's taking so long. I still have to paint all of it."

"You're doing all of this at five and a half months pregnant, babe. Of course you're going to be tired and moving slower. There's no rush. The furniture and everything won't be here for another few weeks." Daphne smiled and squeezed her hand reassuringly.

A few minutes later, they were called back to the exam room. Britton hopped up onto the table and Daphne stood next to her as they waited for the doctor.

"Do you think we'll get to hear the heartbeat?" Britton whispered.

"Probably," Daphne replied as Dr. Rooney came through the door.

"Well, if it isn't my favorite couple. How's it going ladies?" she asked, opening Britton's chart.

"Good. I feel a lot better than I did during the first few months."

"That's great. The second trimester is usually the easiest. Let's take a quick peek and see how the peanut's doing." She squirted the gel on Britton's round belly and watched the screen and she moved the camera around. "The baby is about six inches long now and weighs about eight ounces."

Britton and Daphne were in awe as they watched the baby on the screen, moving all around with its hand up by its face.

"Wow," Britton murmured.

"It's getting so big!" Daphne exclaimed, squeezing her hand.

"It kind of looks like an alien," Britton replied.

Dr. Rooney paused the picture on the screen. "Here are the goods. Can you tell what it is?"

"We don't want to know," Daphne said, looking anyway.

Britton tried to decipher what was what, but the picture was unclear.

"Okay, well, I have to log it in your chart." Dr. Rooney wrote a note in the chart next to the computer and moved on to another live picture as she turned the sound on.

"I still can't believe that is inside of me. It's incredible." Britton smiled.

Daphne bent down and kissed her softly.

"I printed a couple of new pictures for you," Dr. Rooney said, turning off the machine. "Let's see you back in about a month."

"Sounds good." Britton sat up and slid off the table. When the doctor left the room she wrapped her arms around Daphne. "Want to go home and have a quickie before going to work?" She wiggle her eyebrows.

Daphne laughed. "Are you serious?"

Britton nodded and moved her hands lower, squeezing Daphne's butt.

"I'm already missing time today as it is."

"You're the owner's daughter-in-law. Who gives a shit? Come on. We won't get to do this much longer."

"Why not?"

"You heard the doctor. This is the easy trimester. If the first was horrible, then the last will probably be miserable." Britton kissed her tenderly, lingering at her lips. "Go home and make love to your pregnant wife or she's going to do it herself."

Daphne smiled and shook her head. "Let's go."

~

Britton's belly was starting to stick out a little further when she hit twenty weeks. She'd only gained back fifteen of the pounds she'd lost and just about every bit of it was her small belly. From behind, you couldn't tell she was pregnant. Her boobs hadn't changed much either, which she was happy about.

Heather, on the other hand, had just finished her first trimester. Britton gasped when she saw her belly sticking out as Heather opened the front door.

"Hey stranger," Heather said.

"You're belly is almost as big as mine!" Britton laughed.

"Yeah, don't remind me." Heather shook her head. "I never got morning sickness, so all I've been doing is gaining weight. Greg keeps telling me I look great, but I think I could gain a hundred pounds and he wouldn't notice. All he talks about is baby this and baby that. He's so excited to be a dad, he can't sit still."

"Greg as a daddy. That's going to be interesting." Britton smiled.

"Yeah. He can't wait to find out the sex, but I sort of want it to be a surprise, you know?"

"Our doctor almost gave ours away at the last appointment. She showed the picture on the screen, but neither of us could figure it out. Daphne thinks it's a girl because we didn't see a little penis dangling, but I have no idea. It's all a blur to me. These came out great though," she said, handing Heather the ultrasound pictures.

"Aww, look at that!" she exclaimed. "We got these the other day." Heather put her pictures side by side with Britton's. "Best friends already." She smiled.

"And cousins."

"Oh, yeah I forgot about that," Heather laughed. "We can't let them date."

Britton guffawed. "Wouldn't that be some shit? Could you imagine?"

"This is Rhode Island. Cousins can't get married, thank God." Heather shook her head. "How's Daphne? I bet she's beside herself."

"You have no idea. She's dog-eared nearly a hundred pages in this baby catalog we have and keeps trying to get me to go do the registry. Look at this..." Britton opened the picture gallery on her cell phone and handed it to Heather. "We are making the middle room the nursery. I finished the artwork on the walls last night, finally."

"Britton, this is beautiful. I love it!"

"Thanks. It was a pain in the ass, but well worth it."

"Do you want to do ours?" Heather teased.

"What's your theme?"

"We don't have one yet. We're waiting to find out the sex first."

"I thought you didn't want to know?" Britton asked.

"I don't, but Greg will go crazy."

Britton shook her head.

"If it's a girl, I want to do the room in a really light purple with butterflies on the walls, and if it's a boy, we decided on a sports theme with footballs, baseballs, soccer balls, things like that."

"So, butterflies for a girl and balls for a boy." Britton nodded with a grin. "What do you want more a girl or boy?"

"Everyone is saying it's a boy. I wasn't sick and I'm gaining weight like crazy, but my mom wasn't sick at all with me, so it can go either way. I just want it to be healthy."

"Yeah, that's pretty much how we feel, too. I can't believe I'm halfway there."

"Me either, you lucky bitch," Heather giggled. "So, have you picked out the names yet?"

Britton raised an eyebrow. "Your cousin wants to name it Lily if it's a girl and I want to name it Bear if it's a boy. As you can see, we're having some issues."

"Where the hell did you two come up with those?"

Britton shrugged.

"Well, obviously flowers and animals aren't working for you, so you need to look at something new.

196

We went to this really cool website and after going through different eras, famous names, and unique names, we finally picked two."

"Really? You have names already?"

Heather nodded. "That's the first thing we did."

"Well…"

"Avery for a boy and Hayley for a girl."

"I like those."

"Don't steal them," Heather growled playfully.

Britton laughed.

~

When Britton arrived home, she went in search of Daphne, who was upstairs in the nursery. The furniture had finally arrived and the deliver guys set everything up where she wanted it.

"What do you think?" Daphne asked.

"It's beautiful. White was definitely the best choice," Britton replied, running her hand over the crib. A matching changing table and stand-up dresser were on the adjacent wall and a cushioned rocking chair and ottoman were near the window.

"That chair is unbelievably comfortable," Daphne said. "Which is good. I have a feeling we'll be in it a lot."

"I'm afraid to sit down, I'm liable to fall asleep or worse, not be able to get out of the damn thing."

"How was Heather?"

"As big as I am."

"No way. She's only what, twelve weeks?"

"Yep." Britton nodded. "She's changed her diet though and is working with portion control. She didn't get morning sickness, so it's just a steady gain for her.

She's doing well. Greg is driving her crazy with excitement."

Daphne smiled, stepping closer until Britton's belly was against her.

"They even have the names picked out."

"Good for them." Daphne rolled her eyes and kissed Britton softly. "Whoa, was that a kick?" Daphne yelped, looking at Britton's stomach. "Did you feel that?"

Britton nodded with a smile. "That started today. The little alien has been kicking my ribs since lunchtime."

"Wow." Daphne put her hand on Britton's belly, waiting to feel it kick again.

Hearing the sound of her voice, the baby lurched inside of Britton, kicking Daphne's hand.

"Oh, my God!" she squealed. "That's amazing! What does it feel like on the inside?"

"Like he or she just high-fived you with a foot!"

Daphne laughed.

Chapter 33

The construction for the museum was close to being completed by the time Britton neared the end of her second trimester. She was happy to see the project staying on schedule.

"You were right to go with this company," the mayor said. He and Britton had just finished a quick walk-through.

"They do outstanding work, especially with modern designs."

The mayor nodded in agreement. "I heard you turned down the job for the elementary school in Pawtucket."

"Yes. I'm going to have my hands full soon and didn't think I'd be able to see the project through to completion."

"It looks like you've already had your hands full," he laughed.

Britton thought of explaining to him how lesbians became pregnant without an actual penis involved, but she decided against it. Her feet and back were aching and all she wanted to do was go home and lie down. Her phone rang, giving her an easy exit.

"It's the office, I need to take this. I'll see you at the inspection next week," she said, shaking his hand before answering the call as she walked away.

"I was beginning to think you were ignoring me. How's my grandchild doing?" her mother asked.

"Everything is good, mother. I haven't called because I've been busy. I'm actually out at the art museum at the moment."

"Britton Marie, the last thing you need to be doing is walking around a construction site! You're almost seven months pregnant!" Sharon Prescott scolded.

"Mom…" Britton sighed. "I'm fine. The building is completed. They're working on the lighting and fixtures now."

"Well, it doesn't matter. You could still get hurt."

Britton rolled her eyes as she got into her car. She could barely push the clutch in because of her uncomfortable positioning with her belly growing more every week. "If you didn't call me for anything in particular, I need to get going."

"Have you and Daphne discussed the shower yet? We need to book the country club and it's filling up fast with weddings."

"Honestly, I'd rather have at your house or ours."

"Why would you do that? We need a table-style setting so that everyone can have lunch. I'll just book the country club."

"Fine. Don't forget to send us an invitation so that we know the date and time."

"Oh, don't be silly," her mother said sternly. "I'll call Daphne's mother and discuss everything with her."

"You do that," Britton whispered as she hung up the phone. "Damn this belly," she yelled as she missed a gear while trying to pull out into traffic.

~

Mommies

Later that evening, Daphne pulled into the garage, slamming her breaks when she saw a car inside that wasn't Britton's convertible. She pulled in next to the midnight blue, four-door car and got out of her Mercedes. The sleek lines, dark, leather interior, tinted windows, and shiny wheels all screamed Britton, but the car was a sedan and didn't have the Porsche symbol on it. She walked into the house, tossing her briefcase on the kitchen counter. "Britton!" she called out, looking for her wife.

"In here," Britton yelled from her office down the hall.

"Care to explain whose car is in the garage?" Daphne asked, hands on her hips.

"It's mine," Britton shrugged.

Daphne nodded. "Why didn't you tell me you were going to trade yours in? I would've gone with you."

"It was a spur of the moment thing. I hated doing it."

"It's not a Porsche."

"Nope. It's an Audi...S6 Sport, to be exact. As much as I loved my Porsche, that new four-door model is hideous. I actually looked at BMW and then wound up at the Audi dealership across the street."

"It looks nice. Are you going to let me drive this one?"

Britton raised an eyebrow, causing Daphne to shake her head and smile.

"My mother called today. She's booking the country club for the shower and said she was calling your mom so they could work together on everything."

"Oh, really? I thought we decided to have it here."

"We did. We have no say-so as usual."

"My mom wants to do something small at her house," Daphne said.

"Well, they can hash it out. I told her to send me an invitation so we know the details."

Daphne leaned against Britton's desk and crossed her arms. "She drives me crazy."

"You!" Britton exclaimed. "I've been dealing with that woman for almost thirty years!"

"I'm kind of glad we're not involved. I had enough of the two of them when we got married," Daphne sighed, leaning down and rubbing her hand over Britton's belly.

"Has our little alien been kicking much today?"

"I think he or she is going to either be a gymnast or a ninja because there are some serious moves going on in there," Britton replied. "I think my bladder has become a trampoline."

"Aww." Daphne kissed her softly. "How's the museum coming along?"

"It'll be ready for inspection next week. I think they're looking at opening it in about three weeks if it passes inspection."

"That's great. How much longer do you think you'll try to work?"

"I'm thinking about another four weeks in the office. After that, I'll turn it over to Kathleen and run things from here. All she'll be doing is fielding calls for bids and things like that. I'm not getting into any long-term projects for at least six months, but I can still bid on jobs that have a long acceptance process. You know…childcare is something we haven't really talked about."

"Actually, your dad called me today. He's giving me six months of maternity leave starting when the baby is born. Most people get four, which I told him was plenty, but he insisted on six."

"That's excellent." Britton stuck her lips out for a kiss because she couldn't bend.

Daphne grinned and kissed her. She was giddy with excitement when the baby kicked her hand. "Maybe we should work on naming this thing."

"I went through those books again and looked at the website Heather told me about. I came up with a few new ones."

"Cool. I'll go make dinner and we can sit down and look at them."

~

After getting frustrated and disagreeing over and over, Britton and Daphne decided not to go to bed until they'd come together and chosen the names. It was nearly midnight when they finally had two names written on a piece of paper.

Feeling like they'd accomplished climbing Mount Everest, Britton and Daphne spent the rest of the weekend relaxing. The toughest parts were over. Their child had a name, the nursery was ready to be filled with baby stuff, and the shower was out of their hands.

Chapter 34

Britton returned to the office after being at the museum inspection all morning. All she wanted to do was put her feet up and close her eyes, but she had work to do. A pink sticky note was lying on top of her keyboard with an urgent message written on it in Kathleen's handwriting.

Buck Getty with Getty Food Marts called, very important, would like you to return his call today!

Britton knew the name. Getty Food Marts was a large grocery chain in Connecticut and Western Massachusetts that had been trying for some time to move into Rhode Island. What she didn't know was what the owner wanted with her.

As soon as she picked up her desk phone and began to dial the number, her cell phone lit up with Heather's picture. She quickly answered as she put the receiver down for the other phone.

"Hey, guess what?" Heather said.

"You're having twins," Britton replied.

"Hell, no. We went for an ultrasound this morning and at the last minute, Greg decided he wanted it to be a surprise too!"

"Really? What made him do that?"

"He said it didn't matter to him either way. I think he wants a son, but we watched a Lifetime movie the other day about a daddy and his little girl, his heart melted."

"Oh, those damn movies will get you every time," Britton laughed. "So, what are you doing with the nursery?"

"We decided on letters and numbers to keep it neutral."

"That's a good idea. I wanted to do that, but Daphne didn't. I like the theme we wound up with though."

"Me too. I would've copied it if that wasn't cliché," Heather giggled. "How are you feeling? You start the third trimester this week right?"

"On Friday. The little monster inside of me eats all of my food, stomps on my bladder, and constantly kicks me in the ribs…so, yeah, I'm doing great," she said sarcastically. "How about you?"

"I'm great besides the weight gain, but thankfully that's slowed to about average now. It's all up front. My belly is like a basketball and my boobs are huge."

"I'm glad my boobs didn't get gigantic," Britton laughed. "My belly has definitely grown in the last couple of weeks."

"I heard you traded the racecar in," Heather said. "Couldn't push the clutch in anymore, huh?" she chuckled.

"Something like that," Britton muttered. "Who told you I traded it?"

"My mom. She said she ran into you Monday."

"Yeah, I saw her downtown. We had lunch together."

"I know, she told me all about it," Heather laughed. "I think she'd adopt you and Daphne if she could."

"Trust me, I'd much rather have her as a mother-in-law than her sister."

"Is my aunt still being a pain in the ass?"

"My mother is throwing this elaborate shower, you know how she is. Anyway, she brought Daphne's mom into it, who thinks it should be a small get-together kind of thing, not a big lunch with over fifty guests."

"She should know how your mom operates by now," Heather replied.

"No kidding. I think they got it figured out because my mother called this morning to give me the date and time and said the invitations went out today."

"That's good."

"Yeah, but now we have to go tonight and do the registry," Britton sighed.

"You haven't done that yet?"

"No. Daphne's been trying to get me to go. She pretty much has everything all picked out in this catalog, we just have to go walk around the store and scan it all."

"You can do it online," Heather said.

"Seriously?"

"Yes. go to the website and set up the registry. Then, you can add and delete all you want. The product number is right there in the catalog. That's how I did it. Greg walking around a store like that, isn't happening. We went through the catalog together and it took me about twenty minutes to do it all online."

"Sweet!" Britton exclaimed. "Daphne has that damn catalog dog-eared to death. This will be a cinch."

Mommies

Kathleen popped her head in and knocked softly on the open door. "Mr. Getty is on line one."

Britton nodded. "Hey, I need to go take a call. Are we still on for lunch Friday?"

"Yes. I'll see you then," Heather said as she hung up.

Britton picked up the receiver for her desk phone and pushed the blinking button.

"Britton Prescott," she answered.

"Britton, my name's Buck Getty. I'm not sure how familiar you are with Getty Food Marts, but I'd like to talk to you about designing a building for us. We have a large chain of super markets with two different-sized models for our stores, which work great for us, but we need a new corporate office that really stands out. I was at your father's office recently and when he showed me around, it gave me the idea to rebuild. He's the one who gave me your number, actually."

"Really?" Britton raised an eyebrow.

"Yeah. Me and your dad go way back. He's a great businessman and a shitty golfer," he laughed. "Anyway, when do you think you and I could sit down and discuss what I'm looking for?"

"Well, Mr. Getty, I'm not looking to get into any large projects at the moment. My father must have failed to mention that I'm seven months pregnant and taking some time off when the baby is born."

"Oh, no. He told me he's about to be a grandpa soon. He sounded thrilled, by the way. I'm not looking to do anything right now. I'd like to talk about my vision and see where you take it from there. We wouldn't want to build until after the first quarter of next year. Stephen said you're the best architect on the east coast and I'd be stupid not to work with you."

Shocked at her father's words to this man, Britton simply murmured, "Sure."

"My schedule is open next week," he added.

"I can meet with you on Tuesday at ten. Does that work for you?"

"Sure. I'll come to your office so you don't have to travel."

"Thank you," she replied. "I'll see you then."

Obviously, if her father had given out her information with such praise, then he was fine with her taking on the job. This was exactly what she needed, a big build to work on as soon as she finished her maternity leave.

~

"I'm glad you did this," Britton said later that night as she sat on the couch, looking at the destruction of the baby catalog as Daphne sat next to her, adding each item into their registry. "If I had to decide between this car seat and that one, I'd be lost. How did you know what to get?"

"Call it mother's intuition." Daphne grinned, leaning over and kissing her.

"I'm glad one of us got that," Britton mumbled. "I can't even remember if I put on underwear anymore."

"That will go away after the baby is born. All pregnant women go through pregnancy brain. Don't you remember reading about it in the book?"

"Yes. No. I don't know." Britton shook her head and adjusted her position to deal with the baby kicking her in the ribs. "The invitations went out today," she added.

"All right. I guess I better get this done tonight. If you want to go to bed, I'll join you when I finish," Daphne said, rubbing her hand over her belly and kissing her again.

Chapter 35

Britton was thirty weeks along on the day they opened the art museum. After the mayor gave his speech, giving much recognition to Britton, he cut the ribbon. Those who had been invited to the private ceremony were handed glasses of champagne as they walked inside.

"This is amazing," Daphne said in awe as she looked around at the exquisite design of the structure.

"Thanks." Britton smiled. The mayor pulled her away to introduce her to a few people as Daphne took a look at some of the artwork on the walls.

When Britton went in search of her wife, she ran into Victoria, her ex-girlfriend from what seemed like another lifetime ago.

"Well, look at you." Victoria shook her head. "I see Daphne has turned you into quite the little housewife. All pregnant and everything," she said with a snide look on her face.

"Victoria, you have no idea what unconditional love is, because if you did, you'd know what it's like to go to the ends of the earth and do everything possible for that one person you can't live without," she said, raising her voice slightly. "Now, move along before I slap that smug look off your face."

Victoria cringed like a scolded woman as she stepped away.

Daphne had been within earshot, hearing the entire conversation. She walked closer, putting her arm around Britton, as she wiped a tear from her cheek. "I love you," she whispered.

"I love you, too." Britton smiled.

"Did you really mean all of that?" Daphne asked.

"Of course. I'd do anything for you. Daphne, you're my whole world, my everything."

Daphne stood on her tippy toes, hugging Britton over her belly, and feeling a hard thrust into her gut.

"Whoa! I think the alien is hungry. Why don't we get out of here and go grab an early dinner?"

"If it doesn't stop hitting and kicking my ribs, I'm liable to start hitting back," Britton groaned.

~

"Look in that side door," Daphne said when they got into her car.

Britton reached down, pulling an envelope out of the opening. "What's this?"

"Our baby shower invitation. My mom gave it to me."

Britton nodded as she opened it. "I like it. I knew my mother wasn't going to do anything cheesy. This turned out nice."

"Yeah, I agree. My mom thought it should've looked more traditional, but I think it's great. I can't believe it's in two weeks."

"I can. I'll be glad when this monster is out of me," Britton said, adjusting her seat to get more comfortable. "My back is starting to ache. I've tried to stay off my feet this week, but I don't think it's helping."

"Want me to massage it for you?"

"I have something else you can massage," Britton muttered.

"Oh, really? I thought you didn't feel like having sex."

"I don't. I feel like a fat cow."

"Britton, you're not fat."

"I can't see my damn feet!"

"You're eight and a half months pregnant. That's to be expected. You're even more beautiful than you were nine months ago," Daphne said, smiling at her.

~

Later that evening, Britton and Daphne were sitting on the couch together, reading about the last few weeks of pregnancy as a TV show played in the background.

"Are we going to circumcise him if it's a boy?" Daphne asked.

"Yes. I don't know much about the penis, but I've heard horror stories of men having issues down the road when they didn't get it done at birth."

Daphne nodded in agreement.

"We should probably talk about the scary stuff," Britton said, rolling her head to the side to look at her eyes.

"What's that?"

"If something happens."

"Nothing's going to happen, you'll be fine."

"I know that, but we still need to take precautions. If they need to do a cesarean, give them permission. Also, you're my wife, if something happens to me, everything I have goes to you. You'll be on the birth certificate as the second parent, so you'll get the baby and hopefully have no issues."

"Britton, I don't like talking about all of this."

"I know. I don't either, but it needs to be done."

Daphne wrapped her arms around Britton, holding her close as she ran her fingers through her wavy, chestnut strands. "I love you more than anything. Don't you dare leave me," she whispered as a tear rolled down her cheek.

"I'm not going anywhere," Britton said. "Except to the bathroom." She grinned as she eased herself away.

Chapter 36

The country club was decorated elegantly in white, gray, yellow, and teal. Each guest table had a centerpiece with flowers. The bi-layered cake was tall and round with an old-fashioned baby carriage on the top. It looked almost like a wedding cake with folds of white lace all the way around both layers and a gray ribbon going around the very bottom. Britton and Daphne were positioned at the head table, facing all of the other tables where over fifty of their friends, family members, and co-workers were seated.

Over the course of three hours, they ate the delicious, catered lunch, played most of the silly baby shower games, and open a pile of presents. Just about everyone was saying Britton was having a girl, from the fact that she was sick the first trimester, to the way she was carrying the baby high, and even the way she sat in her chair. A few people said no, it had to be a boy because her belly was out front and not horizontal and she'd been craving spaghetti, not sweets. From the back, she didn't look pregnant at all, but her stomach was a round ball full of baby.

By the end of the day, Britton was exhausted and irritable. She'd heard more pregnancy, labor, and delivery stories than she ever wanted to hear in a lifetime. As soon as she and Daphne arrived home, she hit the couch and closed her eyes. Daphne had barely begun going through all of their gifts to write thank you notes, when she heard Britton scream her name. She raced into the den, where Britton was sitting on the couch, bent forward with her hand on the side of her belly.

"What's wrong?!" she asked, frantically kneeling next to her.

"Pain…sharp pain," Britton winced.

"Is it going away?"

"No!" Britton shook her head as she doubled over again in pain. "What if I'm in labor?"

"It's too early," Daphne replied, trying to stay calm.

"Well, you tell the baby that because it feels like my uterus is tied in a knot!"

"Come on, we're going to the hospital," Daphne said before she ran upstairs, frantically throwing some things in a bag, not knowing what to expect. She paused in the hallway to calm her frazzled nerves, then helped Britton to the car. She dialed Dr. Rooney's number as she backed out of the driveway.

~

After a quick exam, Dr. Rooney explained that Britton had begun having Braxton Hicks contractions, which were simple uterine contractions. She told Britton to go home and rest and she'd see her in four more weeks in the office.

The rush to the hospital had been a huge wake-up call for both Britton and Daphne. The car ride home was practically silent.

"Are you feeling any better?" Daphne asked as they walked into the house.

"A little. I'm going to go lie down upstairs."

Daphne kissed her softly, then watched her walk away, before going back to what she'd been doing before the labor scare. Baby shower gifts were scattered all over the formal living room. They'd received a pile of diapers and wipes, as well as a little bit of clothes and most of the other necessities like bottles, bibs, burp clothes, pacifiers, and toys. Britton's sister had purchased the stroller and car seat set, and her parents had given them the bassinet, high chair, and pack n' play, along with an array of smaller things. Daphne's parents had also gone a little overboard with an array of smaller items that she insisted they would need.

After writing all of the thank you cards, Daphne lugged everything upstairs to the nursery, where she began opening boxes and putting the stuff away, checking it off her list as she went. They only had a handful of other things to get, which hadn't been bought, and she'd planned to do that over the weekend.

With stacks of diapers in the closet and little outfits in the drawers, the room was starting to feel more and more like a baby was on the way. She put the bottles of shampoo and baby wash in the bin in the bathroom down the hall, along with the little tub, and tucked the highchair box neatly in the closet since they wouldn't need it for a few months. Then, she went downstairs, where she opened the stroller and car seat box, and set the car seat in the formal living room near the front door. She folded the stroller and put it in the closet, before heading back upstairs.

They'd purchased the bedding set, but hadn't opened it yet, so Daphne went to work putting the sheet on the mattress, which turned out to be a daunting task all by itself. After that, she tied the bumper around the bottom of the crib and placed the comforter inside. Then, she filled the diaper stacker up with newborn diapers and hung the matching window valance on the curtain rod over the thin drapes.

"You're nesting," Britton said from the doorway, startling her.

"What?"

"Nesting. I read about it in that book. Towards the end of the pregnancy, some women go through a nesting phase where they start preparing for the baby. You're doing that now."

Daphne looked at her awkwardly.

"It's adorable." Britton smiled.

"I was just about to come check on you. How are you feeling?"

"I'm fine. It's gone." Britton moved further into the room, peering down at the bedding. "It's so soft," she said, running her hand over it.

"You scared the hell out of me," Daphne murmured, hugging her from behind with her hands on both sides of Britton's round belly.

"I'm sorry. It scared me, too. At least now we know. If it doesn't last longer than a minute and doesn't get worse over time, there's nothing to be worried about. Otherwise, the baby is coming."

"I love you," Daphne said, moving Britton's hair and kissing the side of her neck.

"I love you, too. I can't believe in less than eight weeks there's going to be a baby in this room."

"I know. It seemed so surreal until this afternoon."

Britton turned around. "I'm sort of glad that happened. It doesn't seem as terrifying now. We have a plan. When it happens, we'll go to the hospital, then you will call everyone after we've arrived and know for sure that this is it."

Daphne nodded.

"I repacked the bag, by the way."

"What was wrong with it?" Daphne asked.

"You packed a shoe, an old t-shirt, a pair of yoga pants, a pair of shorts, and tweezers," Britton laughed.

"What the hell?" Daphne giggled, shaking her head.

"It now has clothes and toiletries for both of us." Britton smiled.

"I told you I was freaked out." Daphne grinned sheepishly.

"I can tell." Britton looked around the room. "What's next on the agenda?"

"I did everything, except put the bassinet together." Daphne pointed to the box in the corner.

"All right. Let's get to work." Britton sat in the rocking chair while Daphne sat close by, opening the box.

Chapter 37

Over the next four weeks, Daphne rushed Britton to the hospital three more times for what turned out to be more Braxton Hicks, albeit stronger each time. Britton had finally started maternity leave, putting Kathleen in charge of her company. Sitting at home with nothing to do but waddle around out miserably made Britton depressed, causing her to snap angrily at Daphne, and then cry about it. Daphne did everything she could think of to cheer her up, but nothing helped. The baby was moving all night long, making it nearly impossible for her to sleep and she was starting to become extremely out of breath going up and down the stairs. Her back ached and her feet were swollen.

When they went in for the thirty-seven week check-up, Dr. Rooney met Daphne in the hall beforehand and told her not to worry, that it was very common for women to be hormonal during the last few weeks.

"Let's take a quick peek and see where we are," Dr. Rooney said as Britton slid to the end of the table with her feet in the stirrups.

Daphne held Britton's hand as the doctor checked her for dilation.

"You're about two centimeters, but that's quite common, especially since you've been having severe

Braxton Hicks. That sometimes helps ripen the cervix a little bit."

"What does that mean?" Britton asked. "Is the baby going to be early?"

"Not necessarily. At this point, you're considered full-term, so if you do go into labor, you're having a baby, but most women who dilate early do not have their babies any earlier than thirty-nine weeks."

Daphne nodded, taking everything in that the doctor was telling them.

"Let's plan to see you back here next week and we'll take another look. In the meantime, how are you feeling?"

"Like a cat on a hot tin roof. I'm so over this entire thing," Britton answered honestly.

Dr. Rooney patted her arm. "It won't be long now. Hang in there." She smiled at Daphne before walking out of the room.

~

As her due date neared, Britton had become more uncomfortable with lower back pain and nausea, causing her to be completely miserable. Daphne tried everything she could think of and had read about how to make her more comfortable, but nothing worked. Heather was past thirty weeks herself, so she wasn't much help and Bridget had no idea what to do.

Just when Daphne was ready to throw in the towel and call Britton's mother for help, Britton yelled for her to come into the den. She was breathing slightly heavy with her hand on her stomach.

"What's wrong?" Daphne asked, sitting down next to her.

"I've been watching the clock for the past thirty minutes. I think I'm in labor," she winced. "It's getting worse."

"All right." Daphne stood. "Okay. Let's get you up."

Britton stood and immediately doubled over in pain. Daphne had to hold her up as she carried her to the car. Then, she ran back in for her phone, Britton's phone, the charger, and the bag. She scrolled through her phone, calling Dr. Rooney as soon as she got back in the car.

"I'm certain this is it. I feel wet," Britton grimaced in pain.

"Wet?"

Britton nodded and looked down.

"Oh…"

"When we get there, I want drugs," Britton mumbled.

"Dr. Rooney knows our birth plan," Daphne reassure her as she drove.

Thankfully, it was eight o'clock on a week night, and the roads weren't full of traffic. Daphne pulled up at the front of the maternity entrance for the hospital and ran inside to get help. A nurse quickly came out with a wheelchair and took Britton in while Daphne went and parked her car in the lot. When she ran back inside, they'd already taken Britton to a room. She calmed her nerves as she walked down the hallway with their bag towards room seven.

Britton was lying in the bed wearing a hospital gown with the nurse hooking her up to the fetal monitor as Daphne walked in.

"This looks like the real thing," Daphne mumbled, stepping over to the bed to hold Britton's hand.

"Yes, ma'am," the nurse said with a smile as she started an IV in Britton's other hand.

"My water broke before you walked in here," Britton added.

"Seriously?" Daphne exclaimed.

"Her contractions are still pretty far apart, so don't get too excited, yet," the nurse informed, looking at the reading on the screen. "Who's your doctor?"

"Pauline Rooney. I already called her," Daphne replied.

"She's usually pretty fast, so you'll probably see her in a few minutes. There are snack and drink machines down the hall to your left. If you need anything, press this button here to call the nurse's station. I'll be back in to check on you shortly."

"Wow, this is really it," Daphne muttered.

"Are you okay?" Britton asked, wincing through the pain of a contraction.

"Yeah. You?"

"It hurts like really bad period cramps."

Daphne nodded, leaning over to kiss her cheek.

"Looks like we have the real deal this time," Dr. Rooney said, pulling on a pair of gloves as she walked into the room and looked at the monitor tape. "How's the pain on a scale of one to ten?"

"About a six," Britton winced as another contraction passed.

Dr. Rooney leaned over and stuck her hand down to check Britton's cervix. "You're only about four centimeters. I can go ahead and start the epidural if you want, but just so you know, if you decide to wait and your pain gets to eight, it will be too late."

Britton nodded. "Go ahead and do it."

"All right. Get comfortable, it's going to be an exciting night, ladies. We're having a baby!" she exclaimed as she left the room.

"I guess it's time to call everyone," Daphne said. "I'm going to go get something to drink first. I'll be right back." Daphne stepped out of the room and leaned back against the wall. "Holy shit," she whispered.

"First time?" someone said.

Daphne looked up to see a man leaning against the wall near the door to the next room.

"Yeah. You?"

"Third," he answered. "It doesn't get any easier, at least it didn't for me."

Daphne nodded.

"How far is she?"

"Four centimeters with broken water."

"You'll be here a while."

Daphne smiled. "Thanks."

"Good luck," he added as she walked towards the drink machines down the hall.

Chapter 38

By the time Britton and Daphne's family members arrived, along with Heather and Greg, she'd been given the epidural and was feeling none of the contractions. Everyone came into the room to say hi and give their love before the men headed out to the waiting room. Britton's mom, Daphne's mom, Heather, and Bridget all stayed in the room since there wasn't much of anything going on.

At one point, Britton dozed off and Daphne was happy to see her sleeping. Then, she fell asleep, causing the rest of the women to leave them at peace, knowing that had a long night ahead of them. For the next couple of hours, the room remained quiet and still, until the nurse and Dr. Rooney came in to check on Britton's progress around midnight.

~

Just after two a.m., Britton hit ten centimeters. Daphne, Dr. Rooney, and a nurse were the only people in the room with her. Everyone else was asleep in the waiting room chairs. Another nurse stepped out to go wake everyone and tell them the baby was coming as Dr. Rooney readied everything and Britton began pushing.

Daphne held her hand as Britton squeezed hard, pushing every time the doctor counted up to ten. She wanted to look down, but decided against it, keeping her eyes glued to Britton's instead.

"You can do it, babe," she murmured, brushing Britton's hair back from her forehead.

"Britton, we need long pushes. Hold it as long as you can," Dr. Rooney said as she counted again.

"I can't do it," Britton gasped.

"Yes you can. Catch your breath and do it again, long, slow pushes," Dr. Rooney replied.

Daphne watched the sweat bead up on Britton's face, a little more with every push. She wished there was something she could do besides holding her hand and occasionally wiping her face. "You're doing great, Britton. I'm so proud of you," she said.

"Keep going. We're almost there," Dr. Rooney added.

~

At 3:39a.m. the baby's head popped out and Dr. Rooney reached in, pulling it the rest of the way. "It's a boy!" she cheered, placing him on Britton's chest to get the skin on skin heat from his mother as the nurse leaned over, cleaning him up a little and placing a blanket over his back to keep him warm.

"Oh, my God!" Daphne cried as tears streamed down her face.

"Look at him," Britton mumbled between tears of her own. "He's perfect!" She reached up and he grabbed a hold of her finger, squeezing it.

"He looks like you." Daphne smiled, running her finger over his head.

"We have a son," Britton whispered.

"I know. I can't believe he's real," Daphne replied, standing on her toes to lean over and kiss her wife.

The nurse took him to the scale to weight and measure him, then she placed him under the heat light as the neonatologist stepped into the room to check him over.

"Is he okay?" Daphne asked.

"Don't worry. We have to give each newborn an Apgar score," the nurse informed.

"He's a happy, healthy little guy." The neonatologist smiled. "Ten," he said to the nurse as he left the room.

Dr. Rooney finished getting Britton somewhat back to normal, before pushing the delivery cart away and standing up. The nurse put a diaper on the baby and swaddled him in a soft blanket. She added a little blue hat to his head before handing him to Daphne. Then, she grabbed Daphne's phone to take a picture of the two moms with their son.

"You better go get everyone before they beat the door down," Britton laughed.

Daphne handed the baby to her.

"Does this little guy have a name?" Dr. Rooney asked.

"Yes, he does," Britton answered as Daphne returned with their family and friends. They entered the room, flocking around her to see the baby.

"Well?" Britton's mother asked with her hands in the air.

"It's a boy," Britton replied, smiling.

Sharon Prescott stepped closer, pulling his little hat back to see the strands of chestnut hair on his head. "Oh, look at him! He looks like you, Britton."

"He's a handsome little man," her father added.

"You did it," Heather squealed, moving closer rubbing his little head as she hugged her best friend and cousin.

Daphne's parents moved closer when Heather stepped back, getting a good look at their grandson.

"He's beautiful," Daphne's mom said.

"Wow," Bridget murmured with tears in her eyes as she took pictures and waited in line to get close to her nephew.

Daphne stepped up next to the bed, placing one hand on Britton's shoulder and the other on the baby. "Everyone...we'd like to introduce you to our son, Easton Atwood Prescott."

~

Daphne sat on the edge of the bed with her arm around Britton as their family and friends took turns passing little Easton around, taking pictures with him. "Thank you," she whispered, kissing Britton softly.

"For what?" Britton asked, leaning into her.

"Making me a mother," she said as a tear rolled down her cheek.

Britton reached up, wiping it away. "I love you, Daphne. I'd do anything in the world for you."

Heather walked back over to the bed, handing Easton to Britton. "I think someone made his first stinky," she said.

"Here you go, Mommy," Britton laughed, handing him to Daphne.

Epilogue

5 years later

Britton sat at the table with a smile on her face, watching the two children run around the pirate-themed play set in her backyard.

"I can't believe he's turning five," Daphne sighed, sitting down next to Britton, grabbing her hand as their son came racing over.

"Momma, is it time to eat cake?" Easton asked.

Britton ruffled his hair and bent forward, kissing his forehead. He was a spitting image of her with the same chestnut colored hair and sly grin, but he had Daphne's green eyes.

"I thought you didn't want any cake," she teased.

"It's my birthday! I have to eat cake!" he exclaimed with his hands in the air as he walked away.

Daphne laughed. "He's so dramatic."

"They both are. They think they're grown already," Heather said, watching her daughter, Hayley, go down the slide. The little girl had the same strawberry blonde hair as her mom.

Britton got up and climbed up the side of the play set, grabbing both screaming kids in a bear hug at the top. Haley escaped and went through the tunnel to the other side, but Britton held onto her son and slid down the slide with him.

Easton ran off and made a silly face. "You can't get me, Momma!" he yelled, running around behind the play set to climb back up.

Britton scrambled up the rope ladder, but she'd missed him as he went back down the slide.

"Aunt Britton, get me, get me!" Haley squealed.

Britton turned to grab her and missed as Daphne captured Easton at the bottom of the slide.

"Ha-ha, Mom got you!" Britton laughed, pointing at him.

He quickly got away, racing back up the ladder. Britton was chasing after Haley as her sister Bridget waddled outside, sitting down in Britton's seat.

"Look at that belly!" Heather giggled. "I bet you're ready to throw in the towel."

"I've been ready for months," Bridget groaned with a smile as she rubbed her large stomach. She was pregnant with twins, something that ran in Wade's family. She was due in less than a month.

"You're having a boy and a girl, right?" Heather asked.

"Yes." Bridget smiled.

"It goes by fast, so enjoy every minute of it," Daphne said.

A few minutes later, Britton's father walked through the French doors with a Scooby Doo birthday cake that matched the decorations inside the house. His wife and Daphne's mom were behind him with the plates, forks, and ice cream.

"Easton, look at what Grandpa has," Daphne yelled.

"Cake!" he screamed, flying down the slide and running over to the table.

"This is adorable," Sharon Prescott said, admiring the dog-shaped cake.

"Like mother, like son." Daphne smiled and winked at Britton.

Everyone gathered around the table, singing happy birthday as a flame danced around the top of the number five candle. As soon as they were finished, Easton blew it out.

"Happy birthday!" Daphne cheered. "What did you wish for?" she asked, hugging him.

Easton smiled big and said, "A brother!"

"Noooo!" Britton yelled.

About the Author

Graysen Morgen is the bestselling author of *Falling Snow*, *Fast Pitch*, *Cypress Lake*, and the Bridal Series: *Bridesmaid of Honor* and *Brides*, as well as many other titles. She was born and raised in North Florida with winding rivers and waterways at her back door and the white sandy beach a mile away. She has spent most of her lifetime in the sun and on the water. She enjoys reading, writing, fishing, and spending as much time as possible with her wife and their daughter.

Contact her at graysenmorgen@aol.com; like her fan page on Facebook.com/graysenmorgen; follow her on
Twitter: @graysenmorgen
Instagram: @graysenmorgen

Other Titles Available From Triplicity Publishing

Haunting Love by KA Moll. Anna Crestwood was raised in the strict beliefs of a religious sect nestled in the foothills of the Smoky Mountains. Against her better judgment, she packs up, and moves to Illinois. Unfortunately, she's not there long before she's convinced that the devil is hunting her down. Gabe Garst is a police officer. She's also a powerful medium. Her work with juvenile delinquents and ghosts is all that keeps her going. Talking with and seeing the dead has always come easily, and yet for some reason, she's not able to communicate with her late wife. Anna and Gabe's paths cross. Their attraction is immediate, but they hold back until all hope seems lost.

Rapture & Rogue by Sydney Canyon. Taren Rauley is happy and in a good relationship, until the one person she thought she'd never see again comes back into her life. She struggles to keep the past from colliding with the present as old feelings she thought were dead and gone, begin to haunt her. In college, Gianna Revisi was a mastermind, ring-leading, crime boss. Now, she has a great life and spends her time running Rapture and Rogue, the two establishments she built from the ground up. The last person she ever expects to see walk into one of them, is the girl who walked out on her, breaking her heart five years ago.

Second Chance by Sydney Canyon. After an attack on her convoy, Marine Corps Staff Sergeant, Darien Hollister, must learn to live without her sight. When an experimental procedure allows her to see again, Darien is torn, knowing someone had to die in order for this to happen.
She embarks on a journey to personally thank the donor's family, but is too stunned to tell them the truth. Mixed emotions stir inside of her as she slowly gets to the know the

people that feel like so much more than strangers to her. When the truth finally comes out, Darien walks away, taking the second chance that she's been given to go back to the only life she's ever known, but she's not the only one with a second chance at life.

Soul Mates by KA Moll. Zane was sexually assaulted just days before her high school graduation—targeted because she was a lesbian. The horrific nature of that violation has left her unable to engage in intimate relationships. When Jaina's mother was incarcerated, she and her brother were placed in foster care. The years spent lingering in that system have left her battling lifelong issues of abandonment. When circumstances result in Jaina embarking on a search for her bio-family, her path will cross with Zane's. Both recognize the other as a soul mate, but will their love be strong enough to overcome a lifetime of baggage?

Meant to Be by Graysen Morgen. Brandt is about to walk down the aisle with her girlfriend, when an unexpected chain of events turns her world upside down, causing her to question the last three years of her life. A chance encounter sparks a mix of rage and excitement that she has never felt before. Summer is living life and following her dreams, all the while, harboring a huge secret that could ruin her career. She believes that some things are better kept in the dark, until she has her third run-in with a woman she had hoped to never see again, and gives into temptation. Brandt and Summer start believing everything happens for a reason as they learn the true meaning of meant to be.

Coming to Terms by KA Moll. Sawyer James is a cop. It's who she is and all she ever wanted to be. The job is all she has. To move forward into a fulfilling relationship, Sawyer must come to terms with her past. Sage Carson is a clinical social worker. At almost forty, she comes to realize that her marital problems weren't due to a lack of sexual desire, but rather, her lack of sexual desire for a man. Sage's attraction to Sawyer is an awakening. To move forward, to not spend her life alone, Sage must come to terms—with her own sexuality and with Sawyer.

Coming Home by Graysen Morgen. After tragedy derails TJ Abernathy's life, she packs up her three year old son and heads back to Pennsylvania to live with her grandmother on the family farm. TJ picks back up where she left off eight years earlier, tending to the fruit and nut tree orchard, while learning her grandmother's secret trade. Soon, TJ's high school sweetheart and the same girl who broke her heart, comes back into her life, threatening to steal it away once again. As the weeks turn into months and tragedy strikes again, TJ realizes coming home was the best thing she could've ever done.

Special Assignment by Austen Thorne. Secret Service Agent Parker Meeks has her hands full when she gets her new assignment, protecting a Congressman's teenage daughter, who has had threats made on her life and been whisked away to a Christian boarding school under an alias to finish out her senior year. Parker is fine with the assignment, until she finds out she has to go undercover as a Canon Priest. The last thing Parker expects to find is a beautiful, art history teacher, who is intrigued by her in more ways than one.

Miracle at Christmas by Sydney Canyon. A Modern Twist on the Classic Scrooge Story. Dylan is a power-hungry lawyer who pushed away everything good in her life to become the best defense attorney in the, often winning the worst cases and keeping anyone with enough money out of jail. She's visited on Christmas Eve by her deceased law partner, who threatens her with a life in hell like his own, if she doesn't change her path. During the course of the night, she is taken on a journey through her past, present, and future with three very different spirits.

Bella Vita by Sydney Canyon. Brady is the First Officer of the crew on the Bella Vita, a luxury charter yacht in the Caribbean. She enjoys the laidback island lifestyle, and is accustomed to high profile guests, but when a U.S. Senator charters the yacht as a gift to his beautiful twin daughters who have just graduated from college and a few of their friends, she literally has her hands full.

Brides (Bridal Series book 2) by Graysen Morgen. Britton Prescott is dating the love of her life, Daphne Attwood, after a few tumultuous events that happened to unravel at her sister's wedding reception, seven months earlier. She's happy with the way things are, but immense pressure from her family and friends to take the next step, nearly sends her back to the single life. The idea of a long engagement and simple wedding are thrown out the window, as both families take over, rushing Britton and Daphne to the altar in a matter of weeks.

Cypress Lake by Graysen Morgen. The small town of Cypress Lake is rocked when one murder after another happens. Dani Ricketts, the Chief Deputy for the Cypress Lake Sheriff's Office, realizes the murders are linked. She's surprised when the girl that broke her heart in high school has not only returned home, but she's also Dani's only suspect. Kristen Malone has come back to Cypress Lake to put the past behind her so that she can move on with her life. Seeing Dani Ricketts again throws her off-guard, nearly derailing her plans to finally rid herself and her family of Cypress Lake.

Crashing Waves by Graysen Morgen. After a tragic accident, Pro Surfer, Rory Eden, spends her days hiding in the surf and snowboard manufacturing company that she built from the ground up, while living her life as a shell of the

Mommies

person that she once was. Rory's world is turned upside when a young surfer pursues her, asking for the one thing she can't do. Adler Troy and Dr. Cason Macauley from Graysen Morgen's bestselling novel: *Falling Snow*, make an appearance in this romantic adventure about life, love, and letting go.

Bridesmaid of Honor (Bridal Series book 1) by Graysen Morgen. Britton Prescott's best friend is getting married and she's the maid of honor. As if that isn't enough to deal with, Britton's sister announces she's getting married in the same month and her maid of honor is her best friend Daphne, the same woman who has tormented Britton for years. Britton has to suck it up and play nice, instead of scratching her eyes out, because she and Daphne are in both weddings. Everyone is counting on them to behave like adults.

Falling Snow by Graysen Morgen. Dr. Cason Macauley, a high-speed trauma surgeon from Denver meets Adler Troy, a professional snowboarder and sparks fly. The last thing Cason wants is a relationship and Adler doesn't realize what's right in front of her until it's gone, but will it be too late?

Fate vs. Destiny by Graysen Morgen. Logan Greer devotes her life to investigating plane crashes for the National Transportation Safety Board. Brooke McCabe is an investigator with the Federal Aviation Association who literally flies by the seat of her pants. When Logan gets tangled in head games with both women will she choose fate or destiny?

Just Me by Graysen Morgen. Wild child Ian Wiley has to grow up and take the reins of the hundred year old family business when tragedy strikes. Cassidy Harland is a little surprised that she came within an inch of picking up a gorgeous stranger in a bar and is shocked to find out that stranger is the new head of her company.

Love Loss Revenge by Graysen Morgen. Rian Casey is an FBI Agent working the biggest case of her career and madly in love with her girlfriend. Her world is turned upside when tragedy strikes. Heartbroken, she tries to rebuild her life. When she discovers the truth behind what really happened that awful night she decides justice isn't good enough, and vows revenge on everyone involved.

Natural Instinct by Graysen Morgen. Chandler Scott is a Marine Biologist who keeps her private life private. Corey Joslen is intrigued by Chandler from the moment she meets her. Chandler is forced to finally open her life up to Corey. It backfires in Corey's face and sends her running. Will either woman learn to trust her natural instinct?

Secluded Heart by Graysen Morgen. Chase Leery is an overworked cardiac surgeon with a group of best friends that have an opinion and a reason for everything. When she meets a new artist named Remy Sheridan at her best friend's art gallery she is captivated by the reclusive woman. When Chase finds out why Remy is so sheltered will she put her career on the line to help her or is it too difficult to love someone with a secluded heart?

In Love, at War by Graysen Morgen. Charley Hayes is in the Army Air Force and stationed at Ford Island in Pearl Harbor. She is the commanding officer of her own female-only service squadron and doing the one thing she loves most, repairing airplanes. Life is good for Charley, until the day she finds herself falling in love while fighting for her life as her country is thrown haphazardly into World War II. Can she survive being in love and at war?

Mommies

Fast Pitch by Graysen Morgen. Graham Cahill is a senior in college and the catcher and captain of the softball team. Despite being an all-star pitcher, Bailey Michaels is young and arrogant. Graham and Bailey are forced to get to know each other off the field in order to learn to work together on the field. Will the extra time pay off or will it drive a nail through the team?

Submerged by Graysen Morgen. Assistant District Attorney Layne Carmichael had no idea that the sexy woman she took home from a local bar for a one night stand would turn out to be someone she would be prosecuting months later. Scooter is a Naval Officer on a submarine who changes women like she changes uniforms. When she is accused of a heinous crime she is shocked to see her latest conquest sitting across from her as the prosecuting attorney.

Vow of Solitude by Austen Thorne. Detective Jordan Denali is in a fight for her life against the ghosts from her past and a Serial Killer taunting her with his every move. She lives a life of solitude and plans to keep it that way. When Callie Marceau, a curious Medical Examiner, decides she wants in on the biggest case of her career, as well as, Jordan's life, Jordan is powerless to stop her.

Igniting Temptation by Sydney Canyon. Mackenzie Trotter is the Head of Pediatrics at the local hospital. Her life takes a rather unexpected turn when she meets a flirtatious, beautiful fire fighter. Both women soon discover it doesn't take much to ignite temptation.

One Night by Sydney Canyon. While on a business trip, Caylen Jarrett spends an amazing night with a beautiful stripper. Months later, she is shocked and confused when that same woman re-enters her life. The fact that this stranger could destroy her career doesn't bother her. C.J. is more terrified of

Graysen Morgen

the feelings this woman stirs in her. Could she have fallen in love in one night and not even known it?

Fine by Sydney Canyon. Collin Anderson hides behind a façade, pretending everything is fine. Her workaholic wife and best friend are both oblivious as she goes on an emotional journey, battling a potentially hereditary disease that her mother has been diagnosed with. The only person who knows what is really going on, is Collin's doctor. The same doctor, who is an acquaintance that she's always been attracted to, and who has a partner of her own.

Shadow's Eyes by Sydney Canyon. Tyler McCain is the owner of a large ranch that breeds and sells different types of horses. She isn't exactly thrilled when a Hollywood movie producer shows up wanting to film his latest movie on her property. Reegan Delsol is an up and coming actress who has everything going for her when she lands the lead role in a new film, but there one small problem that could blow the entire picture.

Light Reading: A Collection of Novellas by Sydney Canyon. Four of Sydney Canyon's novellas together in one book, including the bestsellers Shadow's Eyes and One Night.

Visit us at www.tri-pub.com